IN THE END

RACHEL TOALSON

Other Books by Rachel

Poetry

this is how you know

Life: a definition of terms

The Book of Uncommon Hours: haiku poetry

Textbook of an Ordinary Life

this is how you live

Sincerely Yours

Textbook of a Parenthetical Life

Textbook of an Extraordinary Life

this is how you fly

Essay

Parenthood: Has Anyone Seen My Sanity?

The Life-Changing Madness of Tidying Up After Children

This Life With Boys

We Count it All Joy: Essays

Hills I'll Probably Lie Down On

If These Walls Could Talk

The Days are Long, But the Years Are Short

Life's Little Lessons: 100 Micro Essays

To see all the books Rachel has written, click or visit the link below:

www.racheltoalson.com/writing

IN THE END

BATLEE
PRESS

Published by
Batlee Press
Post Office Box 591484
San Antonio, TX 78259

The author appreciates your taking the time to read her work. Please consider leaving a review wherever you bought it and telling your friends how much you enjoyed it. Both of those help get the book into the hands of new readers, which is incredibly important for authors. Thank you for your support.
www.racheltoalson.com

Names: Toalson, Rachel, author.
Title: In the end / Rachel Toalson
Description: First edition. | Batlee Press, Texas:
Batlee Press Books, 2024

10 9 8 7 6 5 4 3 2 1

First Edition—2024

For Ben
I love you to
the end

Trip

We had ten more
good years in us,
after
       that trip.

       You, me,
       twelve days.
We hadn't taken time
just for ourselves
in years,
too long,
not since before Jerry was born.
I faded into the raising
of children.
You found solace in work.
We both emptied
and cracked
and got beat down by the world.
      That trip
stirred something in us,
at least for a little while,
something that tasted of
       dreams
       hope
       love.
Something we barely remembered
but desperately needed.
Something we thought,
         or I thought,

would keep us going
year after year after year.

We started that trip,
the twenty-three-hour flight,
in silence,
like strangers too uncomfortable to meet.
You sitting there
stiff and unwavering,
brooding about the
unfinished job
you left behind,
the job you really hate
but settled for
because of the family benefits,
the job that's maybe
just a little bit,
        or maybe just a lot,
    my fault.
And me, beside you,
staring out the window,
thinking about all
those children
who fill our home with
    mess
    chaos
    laughter
    sunshine
thinking about the dreams
that seemed so important
once upon a time,
thinking about the loneliness

I wear like an
            invisible
            oppressive
            suffocating
      blanket,
twisted so tightly around me
I may never break free.

I stared at your hands,
nails trimmed and shaped,
something I'd always
loved about you,
but I saw a stranger's hands.
I stole glances at your eyes
      blue like the sea we flew over
your lips
      uneven in thought
your hair
      with its gray spatters but still
      thick as the day we'd met.

Such a familiar face.
            Such an unfamiliar face.

But then that trip.
      That hotel.
            Those hands.

Twelve days gone from them,
      gone from
            pressure
            keeping score

       the never-ending striving
     gone from
       ourselves.

Those days
     their art museums
     concert halls
     charming bistros
helped us remember.
And   oh!
     we remembered,
didn't we?
We remembered all the
     kept promises
     the sweet times
     the reasons
for you and me
      us, together.
We left that place shored up,
     bandaged,
something we hadn't felt
in years.

The twenty-three hours home
were so different from those first.
We had plenty of time to
     talk
     melt our hands together
     breathe in the scent
      of each other,
like first-year lovers.
Plenty of time

to think about all
that had come before,
          all that might come after.
Plenty of time
to start believing that maybe,
                just maybe,
I could grow
and bloom
and shine in this place
after all.

But, somehow,
        not enough time.
              at all.

Somehow, all that time
        brought us
here.

Piano Man

That old piano was a gift
from my Nana.
She loved to play it.
And she could play it, too.
She'd play magnificently,
so you'd get lost
in the melody and forget
those bruises on a mama's arm
and what you'd seen
and even who you were,
the melody and harmonies
curling around you
like a hauntingly beautiful soul-song
that reached down deep
and warmed you from the inside out.
Her fingers would fly over those keys
      mesmerizing
      white
      sure.
How I loved to watch them.

She met my granddad
because of that piano.
He could sing
and dance and fiddle
like no one else in the county,
but she didn't know that
until he'd tuned her piano twice.
They made music together

their whole lives,
and we all believed
that made them
              immortal.
Maybe it did.
But it was more than that.
              It was their love.
Their love was just like that music,
       melodious
       brilliant
       life-changing.
They loved in a way
you just don't see anymore,
in a way that is forever.

She gave that piano to us
when Granddad died
because she knew you were a
              piano man.

You used to play it even after
it started falling flat,
filling this house with music that was
              difficult
       like those jobless years
              sweet
       like those allied ones
              soul-shaking
       like the ones filled
with babies and babies and more babies.
I used to be able to see you
in that music,

and I thought it would make us
immortal, too.
Your fingers used to fly
over those keys, stroking
and caressing and warming them all,
and I could feel them
like a soft breath inside my chest
       stroking
       caressing
       warming
the places that had begun
to cool and dim.

I don't remember when
you stopped playing,
but I do remember watching
the golden mist of
       warmth
           burn away.

Tonight,
over a mediocre dinner,
I ask you why,
       why you never play anymore,
       why that piano hasn't
           called you back like it always did,
       why you don't just sit down
           and play.

Life, you say, like that
explains it somehow.

I guess it does. Life has
gotten the best of you,
and maybe you don't know
        or maybe you do
that it's gotten
the best of me, too.

But later, when I'm making
my bedtime rounds,
telling all our boys
and the girl
        goodnight
        that I love them
        what's for breakfast tomorrow,
I see you sit down on that wooden bench
scratched with kid-carved art.
I watch you from the top of the stairway,
my heart keeping time.
I see you stretch your hands
across the keys, flex your fingers,
rest your foot on the gold floor pedal.
I close my eyes and
I wait for that
        difficult
        sweet
        soul-shaking
music.

There is only   silence.

After a moment, I open my eyes.
You shake your head,

your back to me,
and stand.
I read anger in your eyes
when they find mine.
I just don't have any music, you say,
and you turn away
toward the home office
that sees more of you these days
than the rest of us do.

No music left in you.
I know what this means.

That old piano,
the one that used to mean forever,
will keep sitting there
collecting its dust, falling
flatter every day.

Just like our hearts.

Shadow Woman

        Grow
        Bloom
        Shine
I did for a time.

This person
you see today,
this woman
who is
        not so strong
        not so brave
        not so desirable
                (at least not anymore)
is but a whisper of
who I once was.

        Strong
        Brave
        Desirable
I was all of those,
before children.
Before today.

Now I am
a shadow woman,
        shriveled
        shivering
        shunned
by the very ones

who bled dry
        that woman who
        could have been dazzling
by the very ones who
        pocketed all those
        chipping pieces of
        brilliance
by the very ones who
        locked her away,
        unintentionally and
        unknowingly,
        in this prison of
                gloom
                uncertainty and,
                        above all,
                loneliness.

But there is
another truth I know.

        She is still here somewhere.

Run Away

I climbed out of bed today,
drove toward anywhere,
watched some runners
on the sidewalks
that line our streets and
imagined their
much-better-than-mine lives.
We used to run like that,
you and me, back before
our nights filled with
      homework checks
      silent readings
      brought-this-home-from-the-office
          work.

Do you remember?
I still do. Nights
with the setting sun at our backs
and the whole world before us.
Nights when time
      yawned
      stretched
      beckoned.
We used to meet it
with vigor instead of
running away.
Those were nights we
loved each other
for who we were

and who we might be.

So many disappointments ago.

Twenty-one years
as man and wife, and
today you are
unrecognizable
to me.
I no longer know
your hopes or expectations
or the deepest dreams
that, once so vibrant,
have become pencil marks
on a dissatisfied heart.
I no longer know you,
in your black slacks
and your blue-grey
starched-until-it-won't-bend shirt
and your shiny-toed shoes.
You with your rounded glasses
and snipped-short hair
and empty holes
where the earrings
used to be.
You in your defeat.

Long after the house
is quiet, long after
I should be in bed,
long after you've finished
your work but stay holed

inside your office anyway,
because there's no reason
to come out and play,
I slip on some running clothes
I haven't worn
in seven years.

I pause at the door
of your office.
You're typing, brows low and
connected and carrying
the weight of your lonely world.

Want to run away?
Your eyes are mine
for only a moment before
you shake your head.

Too much to do, you say.

My throat tightens
as I turn away.
I haven't asked
for much in the last
five years.
       A little time.
       A little help.
       A little love.
But maybe, in your world,
I've asked too much.

The air is cool and

clean outside.
I breathe it long and deep
and stare at a clear,
diamond-studded sky.

A hand,
        gentle and
        warm and unfamiliar
        on my arm.
A voice,
        soft and unsure
        but distinctly yours.
A tremor
        in my chest.

These are the surprises
I feel.

I guess I could,
you say. *Just let me
get changed.*

So I wait.

For the first time
in too many years,
a smile nudges my heart.

Once Upon a Time

Once upon a time
there lived a girl
who loved to run.

Every morning,
at exactly 5:35, she would slip
out the door
into a darkness that felt like home,
and she would run, her breath
keeping time with her feet,
until the pinks and oranges
and purples of a new day
had faded into a muted
backdrop for a brilliant,
warm, joyful sun.
Only then would she slow her pace
and turn toward home.

There came a morning
after a night when this girl stayed up too late
waiting on a boy who never showed,
a morning when she took her time
climbing from bed,
a morning when
she slipped out the door
thirteen minutes later than normal.
There came a collision with
another boy, a running boy,
a lives-right-next-door boy.

There came a new forever.

This boy
and this girl, who shared
a love for running and
adventure and
life without limits,
began to live
a greater expectation.

Once upon a time,
a boy waited for his girl.

At the end of an aisle
in a tiny old church brimming
with skeptical eyes and shaking heads
and bachelors and bachelorettes
who wished them well on the outside
but thought them
too young on the inside,
this boy waited,
heart pounding, legs wobbly,
for a vision in white.
This boy took his girl's gloved hands
and looked her in the eye
and recited his lofty promises,
intending to keep every one.
This boy and his girl smiled
through their pictures
and laughed through their reception
and loved through the night,
shy and uncertain and new.

There came a year and then
two years and then
one other, each better
and gentler and more pleasing
than the last. There came a love
deeper than the wounds of the world
and a trust stronger
than the twisted, gnarled roots
of the old majestic oak standing
just outside that wedding-day church.
There came a commitment that was
        wild
        unbounded
        grand
like their years-long future.

This boy
and this girl, who shared
a love for red wine
and vintage books
and falling asleep by the fireside,
began to build
a greater expectation.

Once upon a time there was
a baby.

Wrapped in a blanket, tucked in
the girl's arms, warmed by the boy's
embrace, this baby,
        a baby boy,

slept
dreamed
grew.

There came two
and three
and two more, together.
There came chaos and frenzy
and can't-quite-keep-up-with-it-all.
There came a
        yawning
        gnawing
        silent
longing.

This boy
and this girl, who shared
a love for family meals
around a boisterous table
and chocolate chip cookie kisses
and little-boy cling-ons,
began to hope
a greater expectation.

Once upon a time there was
a girl, with child after a trip,
who decided that this time, this baby,
            the long-awaited daughter,
would share her love for
running.

Every evening, at exactly 7:35,

she would slip out the door
while the boy bathed his boys,
into a dimming sunset,
and she would run,
her heart pumping
its life blood
to her womb,
      where a baby grew,
         safe
         warm
         untouchable.

There came an evening when
this girl felt something shift, when
she saw the blood
      pooling between her thighs,
         clawing toward the pavement,
when she lost
      the breath
      the rhythm
      the legs beneath her.
There came
      a pain,
         like a knife
         slicing her in two
      a cry,
         like the choke
         of a wounded sparrow
      a blinding terror
         that darkened
         the day faster
         than the sinking sun.

There came
        a sorrow,
                black
                heavy
                choking.

Once upon a time, there was
a girl who lost her girl
and limped home
to a boy who carried her,
        bleeding
        sobbing
        aching all over
to bed,
a boy whose eyes
hardened while she slept,
a boy who
could not
forgive.

Once upon a time,
there became no such thing
as happily ever after.

Child

This place is old and
full of memories.

I stare and
see and
feel.
Mostly I feel.

I feel
        the blow
                of a heavy hand,
        the sting
                of a buckle's-still-on belt,
        the weight
                of a danger I couldn't
                escape.
I feel
the death of her,
        the woman who loved
        but couldn't leave,
the death of a girl-child
        who left
        but couldn't love,
the death of
        someday.

Someday he'll be gone.
Someday I'll return.
Someday I'll make it right.

You rescued me
from someday, and it
never showed up again.

Why are we here?
Leo, the second one,
shifts beside me.
He would like to get on
with our date,
this boy-man
who could be a young you,
but for the hair,
sandy where yours
is black.
He has a girl of his own,
but our time is sacred
and non-negotiable,
a tradition begun even before
he had a choice.

Goodbyes, I say
and link my arm through his.
We walk without words.
I feel his eyes,
but I stare at the theatre, ahead,
where you whispered
your love and slipped
a ring on my finger
and rescued me
from a hell
you did not know.

I don't look
back at the building,
       tall
       oppressive
       full of her and
              him and
              a child who wore their scars
              in all the hidden places.

A letter came today.
She died
there in that building,
alone
and forgotten
and empty of everything but
her regrets.

I will never be
that child again.

Goodbye, Mother, I whisper.
And then I take my boy's hand
and leave that building behind
for good.

Twenty-three Years

My mother,
            the woman
    with hand-print bruises
    more-whiskey-than-coffee
        in her ever-present mug
    a lifetime of mistakes
        that could never be undone,
thought she could do
anything.

She used to tell me
I could do anything, too.
    Be anything.
        Dream anything.
I believed her for a time,
until my remembering.
Man hands that hurt
every time they touched.
Woman arms with marks
that whispered secrets.
A baby brother,
left to die.
My remembering began to
erase that anything.
Do. Be. Dream.
Not me.

Somewhere along the way,
anything began to blur

into *nothing.*

Until you.

You, with your
see-the-best-in-everything eyes
and your
the-world's-got-so-much-to-offer smile
and your
hope-lives-everywhere heart.
You made me believe
I could change the world,
that the whole earth would dim
without me,
that love could really
    grow roots
    break free of the dirt
    flower in spite of
        the droughts
        the floods
        the years of trampling flat.

Twenty-one years ago,
I cooked dinner every
single night, without fail,
to show my growing-roots,
breaking-free-of-the-dirt,
flowering-in-spite-of-everything
love.

I stir a pot of chicken soup,
one of your old favorites.

I haven't cooked in
too many years, and it joins
a whole list of show-my-love things
I haven't done in
too many years.
But this day
is special.
This day,
twenty-three years ago,
you changed my forever with
a question.

Tonight I will change
the rest of our forever with
a bottle of too-expensive wine,
a gourmet spice cake
reminiscent of the one
we shared that dream-come-true night
and the first lingerie I've worn
in a decade.

I pour some wine,
set the table,
fill the bowls.
Wait.

At half-past nine,
an hour before Jerry
will bring his brothers and sister home
from the dinner-and-a-movie
I paid him to chaperone,
I pour out the now-cold soup,

toss the now-empty
bottle of wine in the trash can
you emptied this morning,
and crawl up the stairs
to our bedroom.

Happy twenty-three
years, darling.

Light

The line between
love and hate is
      blurry
      soft
      seemingly movable.

Last night, when I climbed
into a cold bed
      all the colder
      for your absence
the black of hate and fury
burned me deeper than the wine
in my stomach.
Last night, when I woke to your
sliding into bed
      late
      noiseless
      full of secrets
the hate began to stretch
its arms through my body,
          bitter and dangerous,
like the poison
my mother used to crave.
Last night, when you turned your back
and snored into sleep,
          just like that
the hate was
      wild
      raging

staining our sheets.

But now, in the early hours
of quiet and solitude,
I turn to you.
The peace of sleep has erased
the time lines that mark your face,
and I see once again
a young you,
a you who knows nothing of this
        disappointment
        frustration
        misplaced dreams.
A young you who shines
with potential and
gladness and
ten-thousand dreams.

Dare I hope?

All those years ago,
I recited my promises,
written in black ink and
scrawled across
seven index cards.
That ink has faded
and blurred with time,
but it has never disappeared.
It is here, glowing within
like a dim, faraway,
barely-remember-it
light.

So I do something
I haven't done
since the kids were little
and slept through the sun's rising.

I wake you with a
kiss.

Stair Steps

They sit
like stair steps
on our two-becoming-one timeline.
Jerry the spirited.
Leo the perceptive.
Chris the fearless.
Sean and Ray,
the poet and the party.
And then Maya, our seven-years-later surprise,
our loves-everything-and-everyone-on-earth,
our dreamed-of daughter
who began to fill the chasm
left by the one who'd
slipped away.

Stacked one right on top
of the other,
like concrete stairs
beckoning us
toward the heights
of purity
and love
and bliss.
We stepped on the first stair with
      knitted hands
      brimming-over hearts
      strong-enough-for-this legs,
but they just kept stacking
one over the other,

leap-frogging
higher and higher and higher
until we lost sight of the
top.

Those stairs
demanded climbing;
they sapped our strength
          wearied our hearts
                    made us stumble
so we unbound our hands
and turned away
and wrapped our arms
around the side rail instead of
each other.

How could we have known
that those stairs would leave us,
               you and me,
          twisted
          wounded
          nearly forgotten
there at the concrete
bottom?

I don't blame them.
Of course I don't.
They are color spots
on a mostly black-and-white picture.
My heart is
          better
          stronger

        bigger wider deeper
because of them.

Would I change
how we did it?
No.
Because I know something about you,
something I've known
since the very beginning,
something that will change
everything.

You always get back up.

Garden

If my heart were a garden,
it would not be
     green
     resilient
     flourishing
like the herbs that line our front path.
It would be
     dry
     bent a little around the edges,
        in the places that matter,
     browned all over.
It would be
       vulnerable
     like the seed of its origin
       brittle
     like the thirsty ground
     that birthed it
       shrunken into itself
     like the back your mother lost,
there at the end.

To remain where it is
     vulnerable
     brittle
     shrunken
it needs nothing.
But to
     live
     breathe

                thrive
it needs
                    damp
                    sun
                    the warmth of a
            protective hand.

Leo touches my shoulder.
He is becoming a man,
this son of ours. He is
strong and brave and understanding,
the way you used to be,
years ago,
and I am glad, so glad,
that in spite of my failures
and your distractions,
he has become this.

He asks if I need help weeding.
I don't need help, but I'm glad
for the company. So we work
side by side,
sun burning our backs,
wind sweeping our hair
in every possible direction.
I laugh at him, blonde-brown curls
piling his face,
making him blink against
the sweat sting.
He smiles at me,
a boyish, innocent, tender
smile.

I love you Mom, he says,
and I look at his blue eyes,

     deep

     unafraid

     genuine

and I know
he means it.

I plunge my hands
into the moist dirt,
blinking my eyes
to keep back the drops.
Even if I had all the words
in all the languages of the world,
I could never tell him
just how much
he means to me.
So I simply echo him.
I love you, Leo.

We work for an hour,
the two of us,
silent and separate
but sharing all the same.
And when we're done,
when we turn for the front door,
when he stops me just inside
and hugs me with his
boy-becoming-a-man arms
and whispers his love again,
punctuated by a *so much*,

when we part,
        he to his room,
        me to the kitchen,
I know the garden that is my
heart could begin its
repair.

Because of them.

If my heart were a garden,
it would be
        dry
        bent a little around the edges,
                in the places that matter,
        browned all over
but for a spot of green,
        tiny and nearly invisible
        but significant all the same,
a spot that,
with damp and sun and warmth,
might begin to spread.

The leaves
of my garden-heart are
changing color.

Father

It took me
sixteen years of looking
to find my father.

My mother,
  she was a woman
  of the world.
Men moved
in and out of our filthy home
like the roaches
that dropped from toilet paper rolls
and empty cereal boxes
that never seemed to make it
from the pantry to the trash.
I looked for my father
in every one of them,
but they were too bent,
too tall,
too rough.
The one who stuck around,
who held too hard
and smacked too hard
and touched too hard,
I knew early on
that he wasn't
the one I sought.

My father,
  he was a man

        of the streets.
In and out of shelters,
partial to the drink
that pocketed his money
and his jobs,
willing to give the shirt off his back
for one of his
street brothers and sisters.

My mother slept through
my sixteenth birthday,
but a card marked
my place at the breakfast table.
A card with a name.
So I hit the streets
and followed the points
and found him, shirtless, alone,
sitting on a park bench
with an unlit cigarette stub
in his hand.
I sat beside him.
He hardly noticed until I spoke.

We talked for hours,
both misfits in our own way.
I learned that he hunted
cigarette stubs in public ashtrays,
that he pulled scraps of food
from trashcans,
that he slept in a park
beneath the stars.
I learned that he knew

all the great poets of the world,
that he spent
the better part of his days
in the public library
reading every book on the shelves,
that he'd given his shirt
to a street sister whose baby
had a rattling cough
and probably wouldn't make it
through the week.

I learned he didn't know
about me.

Ten years after that day,
my father got a job
as the maintenance man
at the library, rented
an apartment almost as filthy
as the one I grew up in
and swore off alcohol
and cigarettes
and everything else that had
crawled toward habit
during his street life.
He did it because
he wanted to be a grandpa.

He was there
when Jerry was born.
And Leo.
And Chris and Sean and Ray.

But it wasn't until Maya
that he cried,
        great, terrifying, strangling sobs,
that he said the words
he never needed to say,
that his arms wrapped themselves
around me.
It was warm
and thick
and lovely,
that embrace.

I watch him
from across the street,
leaning against the cane
he has to use now.
He has bad legs,
and it's only a matter of time
before he's wheelchair-bound,
and I'm not sure what
that will do to him.

He catches my eye.
I wave and cross the street
and take his arm.
He leans on me.
*I'm not feeling so
strong today*, he says.

So I say, *I'll be
the strong you need.*

And he smiles.

We shuffle along
          right left right left
toward the park bench
where we first met.
He sits heavily.
I drop beside him.
After a while, he turns to me.

I've missed you, he says.
I stare across the park
at an old man
with a dirty hat
and nearly shredded jeans
and a face with too many lines
for his years.

I know. I shift.
I don't want to tell him
why I haven't been here,
even though it's burning
my throat, this thinking of
you and your work and
how long you stay gone
and what it's all done to me.
He pats my hand,
then reaches beneath the bench
to a box I shoved there
before returning to him.
It's full of already-made sandwiches
and apples and carrot sticks.

He whistles,
and men and women and their children
emerge from shop corners
and bus stops
and back alleys,
lining up single file.
We hand out the packages,
one after another.

Thank you, Mister Henry,
they say. And after he's
introduced me,
Thank you, Miss Erin.

By the time the box
is empty, my eyes
are blurry and wet.
We used to do this every Friday,
together, sharing in a communion
with the brothers and sisters
my father can't forget.
Why I stopped,
        why you stopped,
I can't say.

My father pats my hand again,
and we walk back the way we came
            arms linked
            breath intermingled
            steps matched and steady.

Next time, I'll bring you here.

Next time I'll link your arm
and breathe your breath
and match your steps.
Next time we will share
in this communion.

Next time I will save us.

I kiss my father's cheek
at the door of his
house and turn toward
home.

Truth

Nature holds the truth.

When I am
     lost
     confused
     disheartened
(as I seem to be more often
these days)
the sun
the green
the trees that lend their shade
         begin to call me.

I lie back on a carpet
of green, my face resting
against the cool earth.
I close my eyes
and breathe.
The sun rubs my back.
The wind strokes my hair.
Creation hums.

After a while, the back door opens,
and Sean catches my eye.
We need your help for a minute.
He shrugs. *Algebra.*

I roll over. The sky
is losing its blue.

They'll ask about dinner soon.
You haven't made it
home for dinner in weeks,
but I'll leave a plate
at your place,
just like I always do.
Your sons and your daughter
will glance at it,
like they always do,
     silent
     disappointed
     maybe a little afraid
        of what your
        absence means.

Sean takes my hand
at the door.
Happy birthday eve, he says,
and his smile
outshines the muted sun.
He opens the door
to a table set with your grandmother's china,
a steaming pot of spaghetti
and the biggest,
messiest,
most beautiful cake
I've ever seen.

But what really pinches my throat
and stings my nose
and launches the wet in my eyes
is the sight of them,

huddled around our table,
glowing from the light
of too many candles,
singing at the tops of their lungs.

And you,
	there at the piano,
		banging out the melody.

Fetter

You used to bring me things,
little things,
like a single white rose,
an artsy hand-drawn note,
a journal you'd made.
I kept those treasures
in a box that sits
on my bedside table.

Those just-because-I-was-thinking-of-you gifts
began to wane over the years
until they
disappeared altogether.
I tried not to think about
what their vanishing
might mean, but my thoughts
are not so caged tonight,
and your thoughts
have wandered off to
duty and regret and
everything but me.

Jerry offered to watch
his brothers and sister
tonight for my
birthday.
He wanted you to
take me to dinner,
        just the two of us,

since we celebrated
as a family yesterday.
But your plans for this evening
did not include
a birthday celebration for me,
and you told him so.
You didn't tell me so,
but I wasn't surprised
to hear it. It's not so unusual,
if the last four years
have anything
to say about it.

Jerry wants so badly
to fix us. I wish
I could tell him
it's not up to him.

So tonight, I'll be
wearing a nice dress
and ordering a nice dinner
at a nice restaurant
surrounded by nice people,
and I will be
                alone.
I will have a too-expensive salmon dish
and a too-expensive drink
and a too-expensive dessert,
because it is, after all,
my birthday,
but I will eat and drink
                alone.

I will drive to the park
and lie on grass
and stare at stars,
                alone.

I push aside the makeup
I've patted and stroked and spread
on my face.
It looks a lot
like I feel these days.
Old and
nearly used up.

A knock pushes open the door.
Everybody's eating dinner.
You can leave
whenever you want, Jerry says.
His hair drops in curls
around his face,
and he shakes them back,
a smile nudging his cheeks.
His eyes are soft and warm,
not disappointed and angry
like I want them to be.
I follow him from the room.

At the bottom of the stairs,
Jerry kisses my cheek
and hands me keys.
Leo opens the door
and bows me out.

Just before I reach the car,
you step silently
from shadows.
This way, you say,
and you walk
toward the road.

My eyes follow you
for a moment,
and that's when I see them,
tiny candles lining the walk,
beckoning me
like sparkling stars
that break through
the blackest part of a
too-dark,
too-long
night.
You stop
and turn
and glow.
Coming?

I swallow the tight
in my throat
and nod and join you.
After a few steps,
your arm circles my waist
and you spin me to face you
and then you kiss me.
It is
        long

wild
profound.

And way deep down,
where words end
and knowing begins,
a too-heavy,
too-strong
fetter loosens.

Future

The smell of paint
settles thick,
writhing through the rooms
of the house and settling
into the corners.
The boys are upstairs,
painting Maya's brick wall
while you spend
the day with her.
The day is your
haven't-spent-much-time-with-you apology.
The wall is our
been-meaning-to-do-this-for-a-while surprise.

Chris has the gift of the brush,
so he's doing most of the work.
The others help mix and
outline and
touch up.

Before she was born,
this room was my office,
where I'd spend the nap hours,
the only time our house
shuddered into
still and serene and silent,
bent over my grandmother's
iron sewing machine,
wrapped up

with a blanket and a book
in the window wing chair
or stretched on the antique sofa
with a pen and notebook
in hand.

The brick wall
was my idea, remember?
You chose the brick,
I chose the wall.
I watched more than helped,
and by the time you finished,
you were filthy and sweaty
and undeniably good-looking.

Then Maya began to grow
where the other had
slipped away,
and I desperately gave up this room,
hoping that my sacrifice
would keep her safe
and warm
and alive.
And maybe it did.

Maybe it did.

I step inside the room,
where the paint's powerful smell
turns relentless.
Chris swishes the brush,
and it's a comet.

Almost finished? I say.

He studies his work,
the others eyeing it behind me.
I think so.
He swishes another comet.

Looks great, I say.
She's going to love it.

The boys murmur and grin,
slapping each other
on the back.
Maya is their soft spot.
She has been since the day
she was born.

When will they be back? Ray says.

Anytime, I say.
Let's get this cleaned up.

We work together,
the six of us,
our chatter measured but constant.
I learn that Jerry's
got a new girl
because the old one lost interest
and that Leo's best friend
is failing Algebra 2,
even with his tutoring help,

and that Chris's art teacher
thinks he could get some pieces
in an upscale gallery.
I learn that Sean
doesn't like his choir teacher
and Ray has been giving
half his lunch
to a boy who doesn't get lunch
because his parents are too poor
but not poor enough.
I learn that they hope
you'll stay.

They don't say this, of course.
But I hear it
in what they don't say,
and I wonder how long
they have known about
this distance between us.

The doorbell rings,
and we know you're home.
Maya's never walked
through the front door
without ringing
the bell.

I stuff some trash
in a bag and carry it
to the top of the stairs.

What's that smell? she says.

We have a surprise, I say.
You should come up.

She races to the top
of the stairs,
      golden
      bright
      so very beautiful.
You linger at the bottom,
      stiff
      hesitant
      uncertain of your place
in all the excitement.
When you glance
toward your office,
I turn away.

Ray opens the door,
      grinning
      shining
      gallant.
Maya stands, rooted,
her mouth open.
A rocket! she says.
I nudge her forward.
The solar system. Jupiter, Mars, Venus.
She counts them all
and counts them again.
Her brothers laugh.
Someone has placed a chair
beneath the rocket.

She sits, her joy
flooding the room.

I'm flying, she says.
Her brothers crowd around her,
pointing and
hooting and
beaming.
She looks like a rocket queen,
surrounded by adoration.
Your hand wraps
around mine,
warm and soft and
startling.

I look at you,
looking at them,
and I see a future
that is much like
that mural.
        Brilliant.
        Striking.
        Extraordinary.

Our eyes meet,
and for the first time
in too-too-too many years,
I see a smile
in yours.

Only

A week ago, I got a text
from an unknown number.
It said, *Can't wait to see you Monday.*

I spent two days
trying to figure out
what it meant.

And then I remembered
the call, months ago,
from an old high school friend
whose name is Casey,
a friend I could hardly recall
but who remembered me,
of all people,
a friend who was
coming to town
on business
and had heard
I lived here
and wondered if
maybe I would like to
have lunch.

We haven't kept
in touch all these years,
but I said yes.
Maybe I needed someone
to remind me of

who I'd been
and the promise I'd shown,
back when I'd conquered
the dysfunction
of my family,
back when they voted me
Most Likely to Succeed
because of my place
at the top of my
graduating class,
back when I'd been
the envy of all my classmates
for earning a full ride
to the university where
I met you.

I barely remember
that time,
barely remember
that Erin.
But Casey does,
and that's why I'm here
on this terrace
at this tiny restaurant
in a pocket of town
I don't normally frequent.

I stare across the street,
where the view is
little more engaging
than the conversation
Casey and I are having.

Casey is talking about a job
that's been a dream,
a life that's been to
>   Paris
>   Munich
>   Athens
a marriage that's been in
the crumble stages
for more than a decade.
I don't talk of you
or the children
or the little bit of sadness
that hovers over
and around
and inside me
every morning
when my phone alarm
invites me to climb from bed
and serve breakfast
and send children to school,
because I don't want to watch
Casey's eyes speak
what the mouth wouldn't dare.
You should have been
so much more.

God knows I know.
I know the great
I could have been.
I know the disappointment
I am instead.
The knowing offers its own

accusatory critic and
flogging judge.

You look great, Casey says.
It's a kindness.
I know this, too.
My days for looking great,
for being great,
are long gone.
Long, long gone.

But I say my thanks
and wish I hadn't come.
I wish I had stayed home
          by myself,
eaten my every-single-day
spring greens salad
with sliced avocado
          by myself,
curled up in my
favorite wing chair
with a book,
a journal
and a blanket
          by myself.

Because halfway
through this lunch date
with a friend from high school,
a friend I didn't tell you
I was meeting,
a friend who

is a man,
I know.

There is
only you.

There has always been
only you.

Kiss

This woman I've
never seen before,
who lives here,
in this house
I've never seen before,
found him wandering,
alone,
across a busy street,
headed straight for her door.

He couldn't tell her why
he'd come, but he could tell her
my phone number.
She dialed the numbers
he recited
and caught me napping
on our living room sofa,
my leg marking
my place in a book.
She said he needed help
getting back home
and she,
with no car
and no money
and no time,
was not the one to help.

My father grins
when Mabel, the woman who

lives in this house,
opens the screen door for me.
She has broad hips
and a broader nose
and the hint of a mustache
above thin lips.
Her house is neat and clean
and smells of old.

Pretty, isn't she? he says.
Mabel shifts uncomfortably.
I don't know whether he's talking
about Mabel or me,
but I take my father's arm
and lead him toward the door.
Mabel opens it with
brisk efficiency.
I murmur my thanks
as we shuffle through,
the door catching our heels
as we cross the threshold.
My father doesn't have his cane,
so he leans heavily
on my arm.
I have no idea
how he made it all the way here
by himself.

We walk quietly
back the way I came,
the way he came.
Every six steps, my father stops,

turns and looks back
at Mabel's house
with impossible-to-read eyes.

Do you know her? I say.

My father doesn't answer,
just limps on his way
so I don't know
if he hasn't heard the question
or he's chosen to ignore it.
When we reach my car
and I steer him toward it,
he shakes off my hand.

I want to take you home, I say.

I'm walking, he says,
his voice rough and defiant.
He heads toward the railroad tracks
that split his side of town
and Mabel's side of town.

Home is a mile away, I say.
I'm not letting you walk it.
Because he won't make it,
not on those legs.

He waves a hand.
*You can come or
you can go on,* he says
and keeps right on limping.

And in the end,
I let him
because he is a man,
an old man,
and he needs his victories.
We press on in our slow,
halting way,
talking about
the uncharacteristically warm
weather this year
and the necessity for new sidewalks
on these old roads
and the needs of the people we pass
whose faces are
dirty and worn and molded into sad.
How he ended up
at Mabel's house,
what he is really thinking,
the way his lean
grows heavier
and his limp more marked
with every step,
these are the things
we don't say.

When my father crosses
the tracks and turns toward
the park where he spent
thirty years of his life,
I draw the line.

Not tonight, I say.
We're going home.

I am *going home,* he says
and fights me once more.

This time I don't bend.
Home is this way, I say,
guiding him
in the opposite direction.
His eyes are
wide and gloomy and
full of what I could never understand,
but he lets me lead him
to his front porch
and into the creaky rocking chair
he's had since Jerry was a toddler.
It's twilight by now,
but I sit with him
on that porch
until the first star twinkles
its hello.
When enough time has passed,
when I'm sure his legs
have stiffened enough
to forbid his walking
anywhere but to bed,
I bend to kiss his cheek.
See you tomorrow, I say
because tomorrow
is our tradition.

He nods, staring out at the street
at something I can't see.
When I've reached his gate,
my father's voice stops me,
so soft I almost
don't hear him.
I turn.

I've always loved you, he says.
I want you to know that.

I blow him a kiss,
something I've never done,
something my mother used to do
when the men she'd invited in
couldn't help but declare
their love at her doorstep
after she'd sent them
on their way.
It's only when I'm
a block away
from my car
that I understand,
way deep down
in the place of silent knowing,
why I did it.

Just before his love-words,
my father called my name.
Only it wasn't
my name at all
because I heard

the M of it.
Merin.

Merin was my
mother's name.

Hero

They don't know
what they have done
to me.

Wrecked.
Ruined.
Forever changed.
Because my forever
has been changed.

I had the conversation
with you and with her.
The only conversation left
was the one with him.
I was going to do it today,
our feeding day.

I knew what
his confusion meant.
His brain was growing tired,
just like his legs
were growing tired.
So I had decided to bring him home.
I had decided he would
share Maya's room
because she loved him
and he loved her.
I had decided I would care for him,
all day, every day,

until there were
no more days.

But his legs weren't as stiff
as I had thought last night
when I left
because he walked
those six blocks
to that park
where, a lifetime ago,
he'd slept on benches
and stretched on grass
and foraged in trash cans
along with his brothers and sisters
of the street.
Maybe, in his moment
of confusion, he thought
it was still home.
Maybe, in his moment
of clarity, he chose it
as home.

They took his shoes
and his coat
and the wallet that had
nothing in it
but a slip of paper
with a telephone number.
My number.
He would have given them
anything they'd asked,
but they didn't bother to ask,

just beat him bloody
and left him to die.
If he'd been a younger man,
he might have lived.
But he was too old,
too tired,
too confused.

The day is dim and sun-less,
with a wind that is
howling for me.
Today we were supposed
to feed them.
We were supposed to
hand them their bag lunches
and look in their eyes
and listen to their street talk.
He wanted me to
understand them.
The understanding had
saved him, he said.
It would save them, too.

But today, I cannot
understand them.
I cannot even try.

I take down the sheets
he left on his clothesline
and fold them all, neatly,
in a coming-apart basket
I found in his tiny, bare pantry.

He didn't leave much
in this house.
But he left much
in my heart.
Mostly should haves.

I should have brought him home
with me last night.
I should have seen
the confusion that
blurred his reality.
I should have saved him.

The supplies for today's feeding
watch me from his countertop.
I touch them,
jars of peanut butter,
bags of apples,
bottles of water.
I turn them over in my hands
and think about my father
and all that good bundled
inside his thick,
age-weakened body.
I think of his grip last night,
when he'd leaned on me
like a replacement cane,
and his grin,
missing a few teeth
but dashing all the same,
and his great heart,
        courageous

massive
so tender.

Before I know it,
the supplies are spread,
in our assembly-line way,
and I've taken out
the first piece of bread.

I stuff the lunches
in a box
and walk toward the park
where he died.

It's empty.
I sit on the bench
where we always sit
on our feeding days,
and I wait
and keep on waiting.
After ten or fifteen
or thirty minutes,
a woman lowers herself
beside me.
Without meeting my eyes,
she places a hat
on my knee.
It's his hat.
I know because I made it,
two birthdays ago.

He said it would keep

my ears warm
in winter, she says.
Won't be needing it anymore.

I hand her a lunch,
and she bows her head in thanks.
A man approaches then,
a blanket draping his hands.
Kept me warm all winter, he says,
and he lays it at my feet.
I hand him a lunch.

Before the end of it,
a pile of clothes and hats and blankets,
most of them ones I've made,
rises at my feet,
and fifty-two of them
crowd around me,
weaving stories of the man
I thought I knew.

It's the most beautiful
memorial service
I've ever seen.

They tell me
    the ones who did it
    were out-of-towners
    who didn't understand
    the way of things,
    the ways of him.
These,

the ones who didn't do it,
are the ones
        who chased off
        those out-of-towners,
the ones
        who loved him,
the ones
        he loved.

I leave their offerings
piled in front of that bench
when the box I've brought is empty.
They say their goodbyes,
and I nod mine,
turning back toward the house
where there is no father.

They don't know
what they have done
to me.

        Wrecked.
        Ruined.
        Forever changed.

I never got around
to calling him Dad.
But today I've gotten around
to calling him something greater,
something truer.

                Hero.

Monument

I know they didn't
do it for him,
but when the city stuck
that artsy monument
right next to the city park,
in the yard of some
historical society building,
I saw my father
in its red.
In its one word.
           Love.

He used to sleep there,
right where it sits,
where the city lights dim
and the trees open
and the stars gape.
He told me that once.
So I come here often
to find him,
or at least what
remains of him.

The park bench
is hard beneath me,
like the knot
that ties itself
in my throat
when I think about my father,

even now, after he's
two months gone.
Time has not
softened the ache.
Love is funny like that.

I know they didn't
do it for him,
but this monument
is his legacy,
        swelling from his sleep spot,
speaking to
        the people who glance at it
as they slide past,
        the tourists who stop beside it
for pictures,
        me,
here on this bench.

I take your hand.
We rise together,
arms linked,
breath intermingled,
steps matched and steady.

Love is flexing its fingers,
etching new marks
on the scar-flesh of
my heart.

Spring

My father's ashes
         hide
in a green-gray pot
atop our piano,
where they've sat for
two months.
They have stared at us
as we pass,
spoken into our
reverent silence,
tracked us from one room
to another.
They have reminded us of
what remains unfinished.

They were the
last pieces of him,
and I just couldn't let go.

But today I pulled Maya
out of preschool
and took her to the park
where he'd lived and died,
because I couldn't
do it alone,
and we tipped that pot,
together, watching those
fragile black pieces of him
waving in a barely-there wind

that settled him
into every corner of that land.
Now he'll rest with his
brothers and sisters
of the street.

I said my goodbyes
while Maya squeezed
my hand. And when
we were finished,
when I wondered if I'd done
the right thing, she said,
I think he's happy now
because he's free,
and I marveled,
as I've done so often before,
at the lovely,
perceptive,
wise-beyond-her-years
child she is.

I stare at the sky
      massive
      blue
      cloudless
at the trees
      rigid
      greening
      promising
and at her
      serene
      beautiful

sweet
twirling in the front yard.
She looks at me with
her berry-blue eyes.

She dances toward me,
willowy and elegant
in her childlike way.
She climbs on my lap,
and I kiss the
back of her head,
brushing her black hair
from one side
to the other.
I love you, I say.

She leans back
against me.
I love you, too, she says.
*You're my favorite person
in this whole world.*

I stretch my arms
around her. The sun
pats our faces.
A butterfly flits across the yard,
black and fragile
like those pieces of him,
and I watch it
until it lands
on the blueberry bush
that's begun to welcome spring.

Maya turns her face
to mine, her eyes
bright with question,
and I nod.
I hug her closer,
and we sit there,
the two of us,
until the sun begins to sink
below the houses
and the neighborhood dogs
begin their evening chatter
and your car pulls
into the drive.

We walk inside the house
he no longer haunts,
Maya ringing the bell
on her way
through the door.
You turn to me,
and your smile
is like a warm spring
to my wintered soul.

Roses

The bond between
a girl and her daddy is
      supple
      unwavering
      brimming with adoration.

The bond between
a girl and her mama is
      gentle
      dependable
      bubbling,
(in the underneath
of hushed knowing)
with diminutive slices
of rivalry.

This morning,
the morning I should be
thinking of
      the way
her eyes will shine
when she sees
a stacked-high plate
of chocolate-chip pancakes
      the way
she'll climb into my lap,
moving the morning's feast
to my table place,
while I read her birth story

          the way
she'll glow
when her brothers begin
their just-for-her song
with their boys-becoming-men voices,
I am thinking of
the flowers.

Long before I
shook off sleep,
you'd already been
to the store,
bought your five
pink and red roses
and arranged them all,
just so, in one of my
old vases.
You probably don't remember,
but that vase
is the one you gave me
years ago,
when you arranged
thirty-two roses
beside a card that declared
your love for me,
          that day of my
          thirty-second birthday,
even stronger
than the day we'd wed.
That was the last time
you gave me
one-for-every-year roses.

When Maya turned one,
you resurrected the roses
with another love,
and my tradition
trickled into the past,
where all the Mother's Day cards
and originally-written-by-you
anniversary songs
eased its woe.

She is our daughter,
my daughter,
the girl-child who
filled my hollow.
I know this.
Jealousy is
        absurd

        monstrous

        traitorous.
I know this, too.

I add to the arrangement,
a couple of yellow daisies
from the flower garden,
        bright like her eyes
        her smile
        her very being.
I slide the vase
onto the center of the table.
You're sitting at the end,
sipping a mug of

straight-black coffee.
You don't look up.
I turn away,
wondering if the memory
of all those roses,
burned into my mind
like scarlet fireballs,
have somehow,
unexplainably,
maddeningly,
slipped out of yours.

And then I march,
resolutely, up the stairs
to Maya's room,
pull her warm-with sleep body
close to mine
and whisper in her
hair-covered ear.
Happy birthday, my darling.

Keys

I walk heavy
through the empty of home,
in and out of
      rooms that smell like them
      rooms that look like you
      rooms that drill deep
and bleed soft.

Today
I can barely lift
this leaden head
or uncurl this twisted
heart.

On a day much
like this one,
except thirty-one years ago,
I walked through another house,
toward a never-heard-before sound,
something raw
and untainted
and small.
I followed it,
in and out of
rooms that smelled like men
      dirt and sweat and forbidden
rooms that looked like her
      all split and feral and chaotic
rooms that clutched hard

        and strangled tight.

So many years ago
and I still remember that room
and her
        pocked arms limp
        and splayed
        over her drug-numbed face
and him
        backed against a wall,
        a dangerous bulk
        with angry eyes
        and murderous hands.

And another him
        tiny body limp
        tiny eyes wide
        tiny voice silenced
by the dirty pillow beside him.

I tried to run from
what I'd seen,
but his hand,
so fast and so much stronger,
knocked the light
from my eyes
and the world turned
        black blue noiseless
but for a single thought,
echoing down a
deep-within hollow.
They killed him. They killed my brother.

It's been years
since that day,
and sometimes,
in memory,
the details fragment.
Sometimes they blur.
But always,
his miniature face,
perfectly clear.

Why this memory,
from the stitched wound
of my past?
Why today?

I keep walking,
        in and out
        in and out
        in and out
of the rooms
with their imprint walls,
in this home
where the marks
of our love-children are
            pressed
            mashed
            smudged
into every corner.
I finally stop in your office,
where your computer sits black,
your papers stacked neat.

Your planner lies open.
I've already been here once.
I've already seen
that planner page,
the one with a name and a number,
already read the note,
Marge with the two lines beneath
and seven digits beside
and the lunch time leaping between,
already felt the heart wrench.

An old typewriter
sits in the corner,
an antique you brought
home one day,
smiling contagion
in every lash beat
because you knew how much
I would love it.
We moved it in here,
      to a barely-a-desk-table
      beside a window
      that watches the rolling hills,
when Maya was born,
and I used it for a time,
typing the words
that crowded the quiet,
words that plastered a page,
words that showered
and soaked
and nearly crushed my heart.

The words haven't spoken
for a long, long, long time,
but I hear them today.

So I bend and I write.
I write and I release.
I release and I fill.

I don't mean to fill,
didn't start out trying to,
but I do,
and then I'm
          leaking
          splashing
          spilling all over the carpet
and into their rooms
and into my own,
the one I share with you.

This me that is splintered
          this me that is empty
                    this me that is defeated

this me is still alive.

I tunnel deep
into the scar-darkness,
into the little brother eyes,
into the never-got-to-say-goodbye,
where the slick skin of hate
pulls hard over the truth.
          I cut

    I dig
    I enter.

And only when
the sun grows cold
and the house creaks silent
and the words whisper quiet
do the clicking keys still.

Name

Something else bleeds
from the stitched wound
of my past,
except this one is
      a new stitch,
      a raw stitch,
      a just-been-there-nine-years
         stitch.

Even though
I never touched her
baby-soft skin
or smelled her
baby-scent hair
or kissed her
baby-small face,
I still think of her.
Who she might have been,
what she might have
looked like,
how she might have fit
in this family.

      How you and me
      might have been
      different.

It happened so quickly,
      the blood

the hospital
the empty
where full had been.
There was nothing to see,
nothing to do,
nothing to talk about.

We slept
with our backs
to one another for weeks,
me in my private torment,
reliving
the hours
the days
the weeks
to find something
I might have changed
to save her,
you in your silent blaming,
tallying the runs,
calculating the heart rates,
amassing all the reasons.

She never had a name.
She is my baby,
nameless and
unknown.

Today she is here,
whispering in my ear.
What is my name?

Why didn't we name her?
We chose a name,
years ago, after our first
baby was born,
and it was still waiting for her
after the second
and the third
and then four and five.
We gave her name to Maya,
as if she had never existed.

I sit at the old,
falling-apart typewriter,
fingers of gold
from the window
stroking my face.
I've been here all night.
The boys are awake,
eating in the kitchen.
Maya's voice,
high and gentle,
joins theirs.

I turn
when you enter.
Couldn't sleep? you say.

No, I say.
Your eyes flick
toward the planner,
then back again,
swift and indifferent

and almost imperceptible.
Those are your hiding eyes,
but I have something else
on my mind this morning.

We should name her, I say.
After all these years.
She needs a name.

A shadow steals
the blue of your eyes,
turns them gray.
Who? you say,
but you know.
I can tell by
        the blame that starts to
                bend my shoulders,
        the blame I thought
                you let go,
        the blame that is deep
                unspoken
                so heavy.

I shake my head
and turn away.
My hands find the keys,
and clicking fills the room.
When my fingers still
and I turn back,
you and your planner
are gone.

I roll out the paper
to read what I've written.
It wasn't my fault
in plain black letters,
and there, at the bottom,
her name.

I leave it on your desk,
where the outline
of the open planner
can still be seen
in the morning's dust.

Shrapnel

Comprehending a man's heart
is like
> trying to find a face
>> below the sting of saltwater,
> trying to blink
>> through the sorrow
>> of water-full eyes,
> trying to see lights
>> shimmer through a film
>> of unknown.

> Maybe the letting go
was the first splinter,
>> letting go of the music,
>> letting go of the dreams,
>> letting go of who
>> we had been together.

Maybe I began to live
in silent shrivel,
because I didn't really know
who I was without you,
and maybe I began
wearing my loneliness
like a skin-thin shield
against the black
of ambiguity.
Maybe I needed you
to fight for me,
and maybe, instead,

you raised your glass
to another mistake,
drank deep of secret lives
and new, without-me dreams
and turned decidedly away
from the wound in my eyes
and the wither
in my heart.

Forever used to be
the shrapnel that lodged
deep and held firm.
But years, at least these ones
we have lived,
have a way of loosening
and unbinding
and
          cracking
          cracking
          relentlessly cracking.

I stare out the window,
where a fiery field
burns like the deep
of my soul.

          The name
          the number
          the importance
          of that lunch meeting
bruising your planner page.
These are hazy mysteries

to me,
like your heart.
      Another:
      how much of you
      will return tonight,
      how much of me
      will be left for you.

Music summons me
from the window.
I follow it into the living room,
where the boys sit
on furniture circles,
two of the five
strumming guitars,
all of them singing
a song I don't know
but already like
because it's them
and it's new
and it's here,
in our home,
dousing the walls
and dusting the floors
and soaking me.
I wish you could see this.

Jerry stops strumming
and holds out his guitar.
You play, he says,
a grin crumpling his eyes.

I shake my head.
I don't play anymore, I say,
but he stands there
in silent asking.
I take the guitar,
slide the strap
over my shoulder,
feel the weight of it,
unfamiliar but remembered.
I don't think, just play.

A song fills the room,
one that sings
of you and me,
of who we once were, together,
of who we might be again.
By the end of it,
when the boys have joined in
to sing the song
with me and for me,
my face is wet.

And the shrapnel
that is forever
shifts like a shout of
remember me.

Some things *should* be forever.

Pearl

                There you are
standing at our doorway,
holding a red rose bush
in your jacketed arms,
staring at me
with sea-deep eyes
almost hidden by the curl
of black hair
across your forehead.

                There you are
lifting from your shoulder
the laptop bag
I made you years ago,
balancing the mystery rose bush
in the crook of one arm,
taking in my swollen eyes
and red-streaked face
and invisible battered heart
with the blues that always could
cut right through.

                There you are
ridding yourself of your burdens,
turning to face me,
pulling me into
        tender
        sturdy
        remember-this arms.

There you are
kissing my hair
        the place of protection
and my forehead
        the place of cherish
and my lips
        the place of
        forgiveness.

        There you are
turning me toward
the blood-red bush,
the one marked with a tag
that reads *Marge's Rose Shop*,
motioning toward the backyard,
where you say we'll plant it,
murmuring that it's for her.

        There you are
whispering her name,
a name I typed
in death-black ink
on bright-white paper
you haven't yet seen.

        There I am
crumbling
breathing
re-stitching.

        There you are

falling beside me,
wiping the tears,
sharing your own.

   There we are
two-become-one
as we haven't been
in nine years,
not since our daughter
slipped from my womb,
not since that gem
of great price
turned back to dust.

   There we are
her name rising
before us
like a hope-pillar.
Pearl.

Game

The city lights
wink and waver
in a pitch-black sky,
pointing the way
back home.
I stare out the window.
You chew your lip.
The road hums
between us,
where words should be.

It started out well,
this surprise date.
You came home early
for the first time in
                too long,
tossed some concert tickets
on the backpack-covered table
and asked me,
        with a tight-around-me arm
        and a never-could-resist smile,
to go with you.

You kissed me
outside the entrance gates
and then we let
the music seep
down deep
while our hands

held strong.
Your heart,
my heart,
          beating beating beating
together in an
unknown-but-somehow-familiar
                rhythm
                melody
                song.

I watch the
distant glow of
          yellow purple blue
lights encasing
their memories
in neon glow,
inviting mine to wing
toward their far-off shine
instead of lodging here,
in a can't-speak-it mind.

All the way home
we are silent.
We don't talk
about the music
that grips us even still.
We don't talk about
the kiss that stirred
something deep
and ancient
and full of sultry fire.
And most of all,

we don't talk about
that woman,
    that woman who works
        with you,
    that woman who is younger
        than me
        with a body tighter
        and eyes unwrinkled,
    that woman who touched
        your arm in a
        more-than-just-coworkers
        kind of way
        and called you the most
            brilliant
            charming
            good-looking
    man she'd ever met.

My love is
    violent blazing suffocating.
The air around us
is as charged
as those neon city lights,
the ones that have
all but disappeared.
I roll down the window
and breathe the earthy air
and shut my eyes tight
to the world and
to you and
to our twisted game of hearts.

Petals

       I know
the years haven't been
what we imagined
they would be
back there at the
beginning.

       I know
I have failed you
in small ways,
    like the home-making
    that never came
    naturally,
in bigger ways,
    like the money-management
    that never seemed
    too important,
in unforgivable ways,
    like the music-losing
    that pocketed
    pieces of us
    in its departure.

       I know
I have shut myself away,
    bit by tiny bit,
in a prison of my
own making,
where color

and feeling
and all that is unity
cease to exist.

   I know
I began to wear
my loneliness
like a second,
sticky,
see-through skin
that concealed
every part of me,
especially my heart.

   I know
I bottled the best of me up
inside a shell-of-a-body,
and I know
it took you
by surprise.

   I know
your walls went up
soon after mine,
that you cloaked
your disappointment
in job excellence,
that you craved
something more than
this emotionless,
go-through-the-motions,
when-will-it-ever-end

kind of union.

       I know
you wanted me to
understand you
like you understood me, and
       I know
the pressure
    bowed
    twisted
    ruptured me
until I became
    an unknown,
    a stranger,
    an outsider in this life
    we call marriage.

       I know
I never meant it
to come to this.

I have read your note
a thousand times,
the note that tells me
about her,
    this girl-woman
you met at work,
    this girl-woman
who stole a few of my nights
with you,
    this girl-woman
you never loved

and still do not love
and never, ever will love.
This note
      that tells me
            you're sorry,
      that you never intended
            it to happen,
      that you have regretted it
            every single minute
            of every single hour
            of every single day
rests   damp and crumpled,
in my hand.

What do I do with
      this betrayal
      this failure
      this sickening sorrow?

I turn to the sunflowers
that shiver beside me,
yellow bright
and bliss-filled.
So unlike me.
I pluck the petals.
      You love me.
      You love me not.
      You love me.
      You love me not.
Over and over and over again
until the last petal is gone
and all that remains

is a question.

Who is it you love?

Land

This old patch of land
and its wild grasses
hemmed in by a
wouldn't-keep-a-coyote-out fence
and punctuated by that
still-miraculously-standing-after-all-these-years barn
holds a remember
that sometimes fades
from my
often-selective memory.

In the beginning,
this could have been your land.
Your daddy gave it to you,
wanted you to work it
like he'd done
and like his daddy
had done before him.
He wanted you to settle here
and raise your children
and pass on his
72-year legacy
of hard work
and homesteading
that is all but extinct today.

This could have been
your land,
but you chose

me.

Your daddy had
your future wife
hand-picked the moment
you pulled on
your first pair of cowboy boots,
and she wasn't
a nobody from the city streets
like me.
His words lodged deep
in the sponge of my
trying-to-prove-my-worth
wound.

They stung you, too,
but you made your choice.
And he kept the land.

Your daddy's long gone now,
but he's still living
in the prick of this dry grass
and the splinter of red wood
and the barb of wire fence,
even though all of it, now,
belongs to you.

Maya's footfalls
crunch the grass.
She stands beside me.
I love this place, she says
because she's been here

before, in secret, with me,
and I can see her there,
in the fields,
running free and wild
like the horses your daddy,
        the granddaddy
        she never knew,
used to keep.
I stroke her hair
and slip my hand
through hers.

We turn toward
the car, heat simmering
all around us.
The clouds reach their fingers
to our backs,
like feathery tokens
of knowing.

Your daddy was a hard man,
and he is wrapped up
in this land.
But I still love this land.

I love this land
because it reminds me
of what I once meant
to you.

Weeds

          Sometimes
the weeds
that choke the grass
burst open,
          bright and splendid,
lending their color
to the collective
so a patch of grass
looks more like
a shimmering rainbow
than a stretch
of perfectly manicured lawn.

          Sometimes
those weeds
bend and wave and dance
as gracefully as any flower
I've planted and tended
and raised up all my life.

          Sometimes
they create something
beautiful.

Sean rocks the porch swing
he shares with Ray.
I rock beside them,
in a chair of my own,
the three of us moving

in silent, steady rhythm.

I'm going to mow.
Leo pokes his head
through the front door.
I stare at those flowers,
the beautiful ones
that will die beneath
a blind blade.

The lawnmower rumbles
to life, and the noise
ejects Sean and Ray
from their swing.
They race,
awkward pre-teen legs flapping,
toward the family of weeds.
When they've picked
them all, they return
to the porch,
hands full of offering.
For you, they say.

I guess I don't know
just how brittle
I am because
I start to cry,
and I
      can't stop,
      can't breathe,
      can't even see
for the soak.

I cry for
        the tiny hand-fits-around-a-finger boys
        they used to be,
                all of them.
I cry for
        the holes their growing
                has left in our lives,
        the holes it
                has left in our home,
        the holes it
                has left in me.
I cry for
        you and me.

And do you know
what they, these sons
of yours, do?
They edge me,
like guards on each side,
and they wrap their arms
tight around my shoulders,
and before it's all over,
before the drench abates,
the rest of those boys
find their way outside
and bind me in their
love warmth.

Sometimes the weeds
create something so very
beautiful.

Know

How do I
slide between the sheets
of the bed we've shared
for twenty-one years,
the bed that holds your scent
like a grown-cold candle,
the bed that,
once upon a time,
was sacred pure untouched
by this thick black ice
of deceit?

How do I
keep myself from comparing
    my smudged-with-gray hair
    my stroked-with-wrinkles eyes
    my looser-than-ten-years-ago skin
to another's hair eyes skin?

How do I
sleep with no dreams
when your face is burned
on my eyelids,
glowing in my dark,
blowing cold
where there should be warm?

How do I
survive with the hollow ledge

that is my heart,
the hollow ledge that
bleeds its crimson
right there with my tears
and then
      dries
      cracks
      hardens
a little more every day?

      How do I put
these eggshell pieces of myself
back together again after
      the disappointment
      the shame
      the ugly, unspeakable betrayal
of what you have done?

      How do I

leave?

      How do I

stay?

Even Still

      I try not to watch
you with her,
bending to fasten
the string of barely-pink pearls
you've brought home,
kissing her
flushed-with-pleasure cheek,
taking her still-tiny,
white-gloved hand
and pulling her
and her crackly bouquet of red roses
and her shiny big-girl clutch
toward the open door.

      I try not to notice
the whisper of a suit coat
when you turn back
just before stepping outside,
try not to feel
those tormented eyes,
so sad, so lonely,
scraping across my face,
try not to say
the words I've said
and meant every day
you've walked out that door
to brave your world
           because I can't be sure
           I really mean them right now,

in this anger-place.

I try not to listen
to the tires edging
out of the driveway,
sweeping you and Maya
to her first daddy-daughter dance,
where she'll swing in arms
I haven't felt around me
in weeks, where she'll hold
a hand that no longer
warms mine, where she'll rest
her head, tired from all that
swinging and all that swaying,
on a chest that used to be
my resting place.

I try not to feel
the yearning
the throb
the flame
        of you
rousing my deep.

I try,
but I fail.

Damn this love
that remains,
even still.

Stay

Uncertainty has a way of
    shifting around
        thumping against corners
    blazing its own brutal way

       until

the options
    the black-and-white consequences
begin to gray soften crumble

       until

what to do
and what not to do
and the line between
    leave and stay
become as vague as
    who I am
without you
    who I am
without the six of them.

     You
turned looked smiled
and the warm of you swapped
    old with new
    dark places with light beams
    longing for more with

I'll-love-you-'til-death-do-us-part.

          The six of them
     sucked in breath
     raised miniature fists
     bellowed discomfort
          at all that blinding bright
and pieces of my heart
          pieces of me
began throbbing outside my chest
tugging on invisible strings
that bound my beating
to their being.

     You define
who I have been
for twenty-two years.
          Wife.

     The six of them define
who I have been
for seventeen years.
          Mother.

Who am I without you,
without them,
without the sum
of all these parts?
I don't remember.
The identity that cloaks me now
     vast and unmistakable
is not my true one.

I know this
because it is also
        leaden and bitter
everything that truth
is not.

The six of them
scatter the floor,
heads propped on pillows,
lying on bellies and backs and sides.
You are there in the shadows,
here but not really,
your eyes fixed on the screen,
your head fixed on me
and us
and all my sand-shifting uncertainty.
I saw those eyes
before the movie thundered
its beginning.
I saw them
        watch
        drip
        speak.
                Come.
                Sit.
                Stay.

But I couldn't.
The pricks of betrayal prick deep,
and deeper still
for this relentless love
that burns me away

bit by bit.

   Some things
need to be said.
   Some things
need to be understood.
   Some things
need to be re-dreamed
and re-learned
and remembered
before I can
come and
sit and
stay.

Beauty

The noise in this big warehouse
is a formidable hum,
little-girl voices shrieking
and giggling
and stumbling over each other.
Maya and a group of classmates
huddle in a corner,
gluing furry
necklace-like decorations
to the back of a float.

I watch her
from across the room
with all the other
chatting-about-their-perfect-lives moms.
Her eyes, the violets
she got from me,
shine like berry-bright sun-mirrors
as she drapes a furry band
around her neck
and swishes up to me,
beaming her bliss.

Done? I say,
giving the necklace a tug.
She squirms it off
and hands it to me.

Put it on, she says.

I shake my head
and point toward the float.
We don't have much more time.
You should go finish.

A hand balances on her hip.
The other still offers
the necklace.
Finally, when her face
has morphed more into
mine than yours
for all that staring
at those me-eyes,
I bend. She drapes
the plastic fur
across my shoulders.
She stands back,
head tilted,
black hair springing
across her brow.
Perfect, she says.
You're beautiful.

And, just like that,
she twirls away.

But her words linger,
piercing through
a long-standing barricade,
gliding down the yawn,
stirring the doubt

so that ice becomes fire
and lack becomes rich
and closed becomes gaping.
They are a heal-balm
to a heart-crack.

How long?
How long
since I have believed
in beauty?
How long
since I have looked
in the right mirrors
instead of standing in front of
and staring into
the wrong ones?

What is beauty?
I am beauty.

This heart knows.
This heart mends.
This heart remembers.

Suppose

Suppose I turn
toward the step crunch
behind me,
> where you are
> where they are
> where all those
> unanswerable questions are.

Suppose I fling
a decision
and carry on my way,
or suppose I don't
and, instead, remain here,
under eyes burning
and words unspoken
and heart splitting,
> where shrivel is
> the only ending promised.

> Suppose I leave.
> Suppose I stay.

There was a time,
a lifetime ago,
when I knew this solitude
and welcomed its liberty.
My mother taught me
who I didn't want to be
and what I didn't want to do,
and the desperation of her,

the desperation of those
violent man-hands
that came with her,
was enough for my leaving
and enough for my surviving.

       This desperation,
       this knowing,
       this ever-present aching
of you is different.
It sidles up close,
like a long-lost friend,
and then
it beats me blue.

Jerry matches my step beside me.
Beautiful day, he says.

Yes, I say, raising my face
to the warm.
The park is near deserted today,
though the sun smiles perfectly.

I'm glad Dad got to come, he says.
His eyes watch the rocks
on our path. He kicks one
out of the way,
shoe smacking stone.
I say nothing.

Look at this.
Maya's voice stops me.

I turn.
Your eyes are cast down,
trained where she's pointing.
She bends close to a fuzzy flower.
A bee burrows
inside the petals.

Careful, you say,
and that voice,
so tender and so concerned
and so elemental to my very being,
shakes me
                    until
all I can do
is blink away wet
and swallow throat fire
and fix flaming eyes on Maya.
Jerry squats next to her,
pointing to another flower
where a bee
splits the purple.

Leo and Chris shout
and beckon from ahead,
eager to get to the caves.
Sean and Ray race toward them.
Jerry pulls Maya to her feet
and takes her hand.
Before I know it,
they're banded and we're here,
        alone and vulnerable.
You catch my eye,

and the pain of it
slides down deep.

So much to say,
but the words are
invisible and empty,
pale strings
against the glimmer
of a love that persists,
a love I can't yet tell.
We follow the children,
shrouded in silence.

And so twenty-one
wordless-to-each-other days
become twenty-two.

      Suppose I leave.
      Suppose I stay.

Suppose I
      speak.

Say

The house is hushed
in dream-sleep,
doors closed,
eyes flickering night visions,
hearts beating rest-rhythm.

Tonight I bend
over a puzzle,
joining pieces
to the water bridge picture
the boys began
just before dinner.
Stillness fits snug around me,
like the puzzle links
on this table,
broken suddenly,
unexpectedly,
by a note,
a chord,
a string of unknown melody
that lifts me from my chair.
I lean against the doorway
and stare at your back.

Tonight you bend
over ivory and black.
Tonight you play your heart,
press it into the music
that strokes the silence

and soaks this room
and winds around my middle.
Tonight you open wide.

Tonight I listen
to what your fingers
say.

Think

        Today
the five thousand, eight hundred sixty-first day
you've walked
into that downtown office
to the job you took
      for me and for them
the job where she
      that woman who stole
sits five partitions down
the job that began your slide
toward nowhere
        you turned in your resignation
        and walked out
        without a goodbye.

Your best friend,
the one who recruited you
all those years ago,
called to tell me
seconds before you opened
the front door
seven hours
and twenty-two minutes early.

I don't know what
I think of this.

Inches

The heart's time
is measured in
inches.

Our love crept in
        quiet and startling
while we passed one another
on the morning-dark streets,
while we breathed
our hellos and goodbyes
without breaking
the run rhythm,
while we met
on the hill
between the music building,
            where you studied theory,
and the fine arts building,
            where I studied poetry.

Our love opened
        unhurried and grand
while you shared your umbrella
on our wet walk home,
while I watched you sing
your heart-verse,
while we slipped down ice stairs
and wrapped arms tight
around rails
and each other.

Our love swelled
        fierce and honest
while you picked out that ring,
while I held firm
and wept my yes,
while our hands
found their warm place of fitting
in the forever vow.

Day by day
        hour by hour
                inch by inch.

In all this time,
in all these twenty-one years,
my heart has moved
many inches,
        stretching for you
        stretching for them
        stretching for the eight-as-one
so I don't remember
the small and separate
it used to be.
All of these pieces,
all of these inches,
are tangled up strong,
and maybe that's why
I find it so hard
to peel you from the throb.

But in this house,

we are strangers,
passing in the peripherals,
slinking untouched through hallways,
looking anywhere
but the face
of one another.

Today you were too everywhere,
with nowhere else to go
since you walked out
that building,
so I took Maya
for an afternoon date.
I walked out the door,
for the first time
since two became one,
without those promise rings,
and I could hardly hear
Maya's constant chatter
for the shame shouts
in my ears.

I open the car door.
Maya climbs to the seat
next to mine
and scrambles out my door,
all legs, twinkling her
chocolate-smeared grin.
She bolts toward the door,
black hair wild-flying,
but I catch her arm
and spin her to face me.

I bend.

*Did you have
a good time?* I say.

Her eyes
are wide and laughing.
Yes! she says.
I love dates with you.

How was your ice cream? I say
because I'm just not ready
to go inside
where you wait
and watch
and wallow.

Super yummy, she says
and grabs both my hands.

I love you, I say,
and kiss her mouth.

She kisses my hand
and sings her love,
then pulls me
toward the door,
ringing the doorbell
as we clamber through
the entry.

You're there at the stairs,

one foot lifted
toward the first rise.
Maya launches into your side,
dragging me along
with the hand
that hasn't yet let mine go.
The moment stuns me,
and I stand there,
way too close to you.

*I had chocolate brownie
ice cream, Daddy,* she says.

You had my favorite? you say,
and her giggles
coil around us.
She presses our hands together
and lopes away.

I stare at our connection,
at the warm place of fitting
that is, today,
fiery and troubling.
Your eyes rub my face,
and for a moment I wonder.
I wait.
I wish.
And then I pull
that ring-less hand away
and turn my back
on the inches
that shape my love-heart.

Letters

The birds sing
just outside my window,
but the melodies
that sweeten their notes
are not crooning peace.

I lift the window
and watch them scatter.
They shout at me,
on their way to safer places.
Freedom, they say.
Freedom.

Freedom.

The song
that I am singing,
the other tune
that does not croon peace,
joins theirs in a
stiff harmony.
It says, *Go. Go. Go.*

My bags sit
in the closet,
hidden from their eyes.
Hidden from yours.
Most of all hidden from me.
They wait,

uneasy and dubious.

This room is neat and clean
in a way it never was
before you admitted
your folly.
I know this is your trying
to make it right.
You should know
that this closed room,
this dark I sit in
night after night,
is my trying
to make it right.

A knock rattles the door.
Jerry's head nudges
through the opening,
his sandy hair glowing
in the light from the hallway.
Dad ordered pizza, he says
and steps into the room.
Why is it so dark in here?

Dark is soothing, I say.

He switches on a lamp.
Much better, he says,
but the shadows edge
up the walls,
like the doubt that creeps
toward my heart

and enters,
          black unwelcome all-over barbed,
when I think of them
and all the children-inches
in my heart store.
His voice is man
where he used to be boy,
and the sound of it,
the way it echoes
in my deep
like a silent knowing,
the way it moves me
like a barely-remember soul-song,
binds me, once again,
to indecision.

He stares at me,
coffee eyes gentle with question.
What are you doing?

Watching the birds, I say.
They dive in the deepening dark,
playing their parts
for Jerry and me.

*Dad and I found a cardinal nest
in the oak out there,* Jerry says,
pointing toward the backyard.

This doesn't surprise me.
Since you left that job,
since you've lost yourself

in your music again,
since your afternoons
and evenings, without work,
are opened wide,
you and the kids
spend hours of time together.
This is good,
when I think of
those hidden bags.

Are you hungry? Jerry says,
and I feel his eyes
warming my face.

I haven't been hungry in months,
not since you scrawled
that confession
on college-ruled notebook paper,
but I face him
and grab both his hands.
I'll be down in a minute, I say.
He nods and moves away.
I turn back
toward the window,
so his embrace surprises me.

I love you, Mom, he says,
and after a minute of tight,
his arms fall to his sides,
and he slips out the door,
shutting it soft behind him.

I stumble toward the bed,
my eyes stinging with blur.
On the way, my foot twists
on something cold and hard
beneath the bed.
I bend to the floor,
wet rinsing my cheeks.
It's an old Christmas ornament,
one that should have been
packed up months ago.
My step snapped it in two,
so the word it used to be
is no more.

But the letters that remain,
the letters that are incomplete
and damaged
and jagged with break,
mean something
far greater to me
than the peace it used to proclaim.

Phil. Erin, they say. *Stay.*

Known

    If I had known
what tomorrow held
in its fiery hands,
I would have
burned that confession
instead of burying it
beneath my neatly folded intimates,
where my hands
would touch it,
where my eyes
would read it,
over and over and over again,
where my heart
would grip the fury,
the shame,
the betrayal of it.

    If I had known
what tomorrow held
in its fiery hands,
I would have believed
that last petal.
He loves me.

    If I had known
what tomorrow held
in its fiery hands,
I would have watched her,
    shimmering and shining

in her princess dress,
with you,
        debonair and darkly mysterious
in that barely-worn suit coat
I bought you
on our fifth anniversary,
and I would have
smiled my devotion
and snapped my
one-thousand pictures
before you turned your backs
and waltzed out that door
toward the dance
she'd been waiting for
her whole life.

        If I had known
what tomorrow held,
I would have boxed up
every room in this house
and carted every last photograph,
every last sock,
every last music piece,
single-handedly,
to that piece of land
that she loved so much,
the piece of land
that spoke of love
and sacrifice
and courage
in its dried-out grass
and hardly-standing barn.

If I had known
what tomorrow held,
I would have bought those roses,
the ones that marked
her five years, myself
instead of begrudging you
the giving with my
silent, bitter score.

If I had known
what tomorrow held,
I would have joined you
in the backyard,
where the boys
found that cardinal,
where she touched
those tiny eggs,
and I would have laughed
and teased
and nearly burst
for the fullness of our eight
instead of withering
in my dark.

If I had known
I would have kept my hand
warm and firm in yours
instead of pulling
too quickly away
and turning my back
so her eyes,

those blueberry eyes,
turned dusk with the woe
of our disconnection
when she skipped back
into the room.

      If I had known
I would have remained here,
in her sleep-quiet room,
where my hands brush
her hair and yours her face,
and I would have let
those brushing hands
bind together,
speaking a knowing too great for words,
and I would have pulled you
to our bed,
to our too-cold covers,
to the warm our bodies would bleed
beneath them,
on this last night of life
as we have lived it.

      If I had known
I would have gripped stronger
and spoken earlier
and forgiven better.

But tomorrow
never makes known
what it holds in its
fiery hands.

Snapshots

I would remember
only jagged splinters
of the day,
like snapshots
of petrified time.

Maya, asleep in her bed.
You, across the table,
blowing on black coffee.
The boys, piling out the door,
racing toward the bus.
Me, blowing my goodbyes,
empty tea cup in hand.
You, eyes soggy,
voice unsteady,
words like breath pants:
>   *I'm so sorry.*
Me, sucking in leaden air,
too afraid to speak,
too afraid to do this
right now.
You, trying again:
>   *I've only ever loved you.*
Me, words like
too-sharp spikes:
>   *Your way of love…*
and no more.
You, cracking in sorrow:
>   *I know. I've let you down.*

Maya, suddenly there in the kitchen,
rubbing sleep-heavy eyes.
Me, turning my back,
heaving open the refrigerator,
dismissing you
for the task of her breakfast.
You, lurching
toward the door
on legs of regret.
Maya, watching you go,
looking at me,
asking in her sweet angel voice:
Mama, do you love Daddy?
just before the door
groaned open.
Me, grappling for words
I wouldn't find
in your leaving pause.
Maya, eyes spilling
after the slam shut.
Me, slipping out,
slipping away,
slipping back into my dark.

Those words
I did not say,
festering like
acid sores on a
ruined heart.

Forget

And then the evening
I would never,
ever forget,
not in all my life.

She stops
for a ladybug
making its way
across a mountainous
rock path,
twisting and turning,
climbing and sliding
in a scurry toward safer.
She wants to help it
get to the grass,
where it belongs.
It clings to the
finger she offers,
and she drops it in green.

You and the boys
have gone ahead,
splashing into
the sun-warm water.
One of the boys
calls her name.
I touch her back
where she bends in the grass.
Your brothers are waiting, I say.

She grins,
and then she's racing
toward the huddle of all of you,
cutting the glass-smooth water
with bare-chested bodies.
You are there,
looking young and strong
like your sons.
Maya stands at the edge,
waiting until you grab her hand
to tuck into her jump.
She does not fear water,
but she knows the rules.

I sink into a shaded seat
beside the pool.
A bird explores the underneath,
stripe-shadowed by a lawn chair
further down the line.
It watches them like I watch,
     head cocked,
      brown-gray body tensed
        and ready for flight.
A second bird calls
from somewhere
above the clubhouse,
and the first
spreads its wings
and lifts toward answer.

The wind sighs
in my ear,

but I cannot hear
the secrets it whispers
above the noise of their shouting.

Cold water sprays my feet.
Maya giggles and launches herself
back toward her brothers,
her arms moving
the way you taught her.
You watch from behind,
following her toward the deep.
It's so cold! she shrieks
and the boys hoot with laughter.

The pool shimmers,
wet fingers rocking
in a steady rhythm of soothe,
lapping against
the walls of cement,
turning my eyelids
heavy and black.

I dream of them.
Leo, four, waiting for his turn
to toss the pool toy
you've just retrieved
from the bottom of the water,
saying, *Throw it to me, Daddy.*
Jerry, six, refusing to learn
to swim until he's eighteen.
Chris, two, hugging the gate,
where fear confined him

because of an early
lost-his-footing fall
into too-deep water.
Chris and Ray, one,
gliding side by side
on baby floats,
me between them.

I dream of life before Maya.

I wake knowing
something is wrong.
My legs lift me,
walk me toward
the deep end,
turn me right around again.

I don't know,
Leo is saying,
his eyes wild and frantic.

I count them.
Five where six should be.
One missing.
One girl missing.

How long? you say,
and your swim strokes
are strong,
but your voice shivers
like the surface
of that water.

A minute? Chris says.
He's out of the pool,
walking the perimeter.

This water is clear.
We should be able to see her.

And suddenly I know.
Suddenly I'm running.
Suddenly I can barely breathe.
My heart slams toward my stomach
as I follow the sidewalk
to the shallow pool
where they used to play
before they knew how to swim.
She knows how to swim.

She knows how to swim.

I slip, my knee crashing hard
against rock,
so Jerry beats me to the water,
but I have already seen
what is there at the bottom,
the black hair
that swells through clear
like a suffocating smoke cloud.
And then Jerry
is breaking the calm,
pulling her up,
laying her down

like a costly porcelain doll
on the path beside the rock
where she stood,
not an hour ago,
bending over that ladybug.

He leans over her,
        pumping breathing,
        pumping breathing,
never stopping,
on and on and on and on.
He is desperate to save her.

Sirens blast in the distance,
like muted echoes
in a cave of black,
and someone's hands
clench my arms,
but they cannot keep me
from falling.
Wails join the sirens
like a soul-wrenching dirge
that tells of a life
too-soon gone.

I turn away
from the gray
and the blue
and the eyes
that stare up at a sky
she cannot see.

Colors

I used to think that sorrow,
with its violent hollowing,
its unbearable ache,
its everywhere chasm,
would bleed the colors
from the world,
turn them black
and gray
and all over dark.
Now I know better.

This sorrow sees color,
all the blues and greens
and pinks and yellows
a heart could ever want.
They're just all mixed up,
skidding one into another,
like a watercolor painting
left too long in the rain.

The colors in my world
are weeping with me.

Gap

I see her everywhere.
That watermelon seed
she planted
in the middle
of our back yard,
the one that's just
begun to sprout its green,
the one I scolded her
for burying,
    the one I can't bring myself
    to uproot.

That birdhouse
rocking in the wind,
the one she gave me
for last year's Mother's Day,
the one no bird
has ever used
because the wood is sharp
and crooked
and crack-filled
but also perfect
because her hands made it,
    the one I can't bring myself
    to pull down.

That purple shutter
splitting the silver
of your work shed,

the one she painted
the color she liked best,
the one she used to swing
open wide for a wave
when she'd joined
your work inside,
      the one I can't bring myself
      to paint black
      like the color of loss,
      the color of nothing,
      the color of my heart
      where she used to be.

The wind beats that shutter
against the side of your shed,
and every crack
feels like new fissures in me.
I stand there for minutes
or hours
or maybe the entire,
light-less day
because time means nothing
in the warp of grief.
I watch that purple shutter
and listen to its cracking
and feel, way down deep,
its splinters wounding me
again and again and again.
And then it moves
in a way too calculated
for the reckless wind whip,
opening unexpectedly

but recognizably.
My heart flips
when I see who stares
right back at me.

There,
standing in the gap,
is you.

Goodbye

Today I walked
ten miles
before we would mark
the death of her living
in a too-chilly church building
full of people
I might not ever
be ready to see again,
and in my aimless wanderings,
in my outrunning-grief attempt,
in my trying to forget
the dark of the afternoon,
I collected pictures,
evidence that this world
carries on its turning
even while my world,
           a world without her,
lies frozen.

Click. A little boy
in a wooden wagon,
his mother close by
the front wheel,
a mother walking backwards
because that's where he,
her beloved, is,
a mother who throws her head
to the cloudless sky
when his little-boy voice

begins its dance
in the wind
and her big-girl voice
skips around it.

Click. A cat,
like the one she loved
and lost last year,
lounging in the cool
of a pickup truck shadow,
a cat rolling on pavement,
a cat watching
with eyes aware
and body poised for flight
but for one paw lifted up,
raised in feline hello.

Click. A little girl
on unsteady legs
and bare feet,
clutching an iron gate,
a little girl with
sagging-to-knees diaper
and bruises climbing her body,
a little girl disappearing
into an open door,
into a house chipped and leaning,
into a world that plays
with fire and ice
and kerosene jugs
sitting too close
to gaping doorways.

Normally we would have
shared these pictures
during our late afternoon walk,
she and I.
Normally she would have
remembered for me
the color of that wagon,
the exact location of that cat,
the face of that child.
Normally she would have
recounted our findings to you,
second by second,
face by face,
color by color,
during a dinner set
for a party of eight.

These pictures,
        without her,
smudge and fade
and lose their vibrancy,
much like my world
        without her,
smudges and fades
and loses its vibrancy.

I slide through
the front door,
trying not to look
at the doorbell
you dismantled

the night she turned cold.
You and the boys
are waiting,
black suits buttoned,
gray ties knotted,
hands in pockets.
Your eyes,
all twelve of them,
look my way,
and the relief that watches me
wrenches the breath
from my lungs
and pours anger drops
down my cheeks.

Tell me, please:
What, in this frozen, smudging,
hollowed-out life without her,
could bring such relief
to the faces of you,
the ones who say
you loved her
as much as I?

And then,
sudden and unexpected
like the slip on the sidewalk
that hurled her into faint-sleep
and three-feet-deep water
and forever black,
I know.

Here is what
I want all of you to know:
I will always come back.

So I open my arms
as wide as I can,
and I say something
that is nothing at all,
and they come,
all of them,
with crumpled faces
and spilling eyes
and shuffling steps,
and I know
this isn't just about me
and it isn't just about her
and it isn't just about this
chasm of sad
bending our backs.

You move with them,
flanking them from behind,
and together,
we hedge them
and hold them
and hem them
within our arms.

And when the water stops its leaking
and the shudders stop their lashing
and the voices stop their breaking,
we make our way,

together, toward
the place of goodbye.

Road

A road
>   long and narrow
>   and twisting toward unknown
winds its way
to the church
where she is waiting.

A road
>   long and narrow
>   and twisting toward unknown
winds its way
to the deep of
my heart.

This road is one
I never wanted
to travel.
All that waiting
for all those years,
and then promise became
a tiny, shrieking,
black-haired beauty
of silk skin and wrinkles.
You got your princess.
I got my forever-friend.

It was easy to imagine
who she might become.
I had only to look

in the mirror, at Leo,
at that portrait of your mother
hanging in our hall.
She was all of us.
Same porcelain-doll skin.
Same raven hair.
Same blueberry eyes.

What bends and curves
this never-wanted-to-travel road?
It is not
the sky-scraping trees
or the ravines
that gurgle through green
or the natural way of things.
   Why this road, so ugly?
   Why this twist, so sharp?
   Why this reality, so ruthless?

The sun gleams
off the road,
and its brilliance blinds us.
You blink, again and again,
trying to clear
the intensity
from your eyes
because it feels wrong
on this day
of all days.

Ahead, a steeple reaches
toward cotton ball clouds.

Someone sniffs in the back,
but I don't turn.
To turn would be to notice
her empty seat,
there between Sean and Ray.
To turn would be to see.
To turn would be to know.

The crackling of the gravel
beneath our tires
sounds much like
the split pieces of my heart
clattering in my chest.
The seven of us
climb from our seats
and turn toward
the dirty white church,
where we'll see,
once more,
her porcelain-doll skin
and raven hair
but no blueberry eyes.

I darken those
heavy doors alone.
You and the boys
wait outside,
wait with her case,
wait to parade her
down an aisle
lined with brown carpet
and yellow rose petals,

something I'd envisioned
for another day,
a happier day,
a love day.
I move past family and friends
uncomfortable in their seats.
They murmur their condolences,
but I know that secretly
they are thankful
my life is not their own.

My tears begin
when the music
we all know by heart begins,
when her sweet voice
wings toward the ceiling
of that church,
rising and falling
in the melody of songs
she'd composed on our computer
for you
and for me
and for her brothers.
And then the smallest,
heaviest case
I've ever seen
creeps down that aisle,
gripped tight in the hands
of you and them,
and is set down
between the lily plants
and rose bushes

Leo potted for her
on this farewell day.
Somewhere in the middle
of her singing
and your carrying
and Jerry's speaking
and Chris's painting
and Sean's reading
and Ray's poetry,
somewhere in the middle of it all,
your arm slides
around my shoulders
and our heads bow
to touching
and our hands knot
together.

And when it's all over,
we turn back
the way we came,
down the so long
and so narrow
and so full-of-twists road,
the place none of us
ever wanted
to go.

Unspoken

Your sister
follows us home.

She is a smaller version
of your mother,
so looking at her
passing through our doorway
is like watching grown Maya
come for a visit.
I blink water
from my eyes
and stumble in behind her.
She has stopped
just inside the doorway,
and I know what she sees.
Paper mounds on the
dining room table,
a weak attempt
to keep up with the world
that spins on relentlessly.
Pool towels striping the floor,
mirroring our desperate flight
to a room where she
never woke.
Maya's ruby backpack,
propped beside the front door
where she left it
that day.

Your sister turns to me.
I'll stay a few weeks, she says,
and all I can do
is squeeze Jerry's hand in mine
and dip my head
and stagger up stairs
that lead to a bed
sitting in darkness.

When I wake,
the sun is low in the sky.
I pull back the curtain
and stare out a window
at the weakening light,
and only when the diluted rays
have pricked the sleep
from my eyes
do I move back down the stairs.
The six of you sit
in a living room
no longer striped
with pool towels,
silent and frozen
like boy-man sculptures
hardened by misery.
You stand when I move into view.
Your eyes are weak and troubled.
You gesture toward the kitchen,
where your sister stands,
her back to us.

When she turns,

she looks at me
and nods toward the counter.
I took the liberty
of cleaning up a little, she says,
and, for a moment,
I think she's talking
about the no-longer-stacked papers
and the no-longer-striping towels
and the no-longer-propped backpack.
Then I see them,
the bottle caps
and the still-dirty rocks
and the dried-out leaves,
trash-treasures from Maya's room,
a place we haven't gone
since she left us.

A surge of fury slaps me,
swift and breath-snatching.
After all these years
of unreturned calls
and tucked-away secrets
and voluntary slipping
from the significant place
she used to hold in our lives,
this woman
        your sister
    who crossed the line
    to our side when your father
    held that land over your head,
    who carried my
    pink-tipped rose bouquet

back down the aisle
on our union day,
who knew me and loved me
like a sister-friend
for all those years before the day,
who ten years ago
married a man
who didn't know any of us
and didn't care to know
has gone too far.

I grip the bottle cap basket
in a hand
that is white with intention,
and I plunge the other
into the bristly metal,
feeling their puncture
on fingers clenched tight.
And then, as suddenly
as I've grabbed them,
I hurl them,
that handful of bottle caps
she used to collect
on our late afternoon walks,
when we'd stroll hand-in-hand,
pulling behind us
that old beat-up wagon,
the one that carried, on one side,
a trash bag for the litter,
and, on the other,
a basket for her treasures.
We'd make our way

down those streets,
bending and cleaning and sorting.
Leo's love for the earth
was her love,
just like Jerry's love for music
and Chris's love for art
and Sean's and Ray's love
for books and poetry
were her loves.
She was the best of us all.
You
      me
            them.

She connected us in her life.
She connects us still in her death,
and I know this
because after those caps
have grazed your sister's face,
we stand there
      the seven of us
staring at her
in a kitchen that smells
of tomato and garlic and cilantro.
Your sister stares back,
her eyes wide, unblinking.
Bottle caps litter
the tile around her feet,
some of them still spinning.
She looks at me
      then you
            then them

and she knows
what hangs between us,
                    unspoken.

Your hands cup mine,
where dots of crimson swell.
My words are barely a whisper.
I'm sorry, Lily, I say.

We'll give it time, she says
in a voice drawn taut.
But I know the truth of it.
No matter how many days
or weeks or months pass us,
these treasures,
the ones she pulled from her world,
will remain to fill our home
with her presence.

Your sister moves
toward the pot on the stove,
stirring a bright-red soup
we probably won't eat this night.
She means well,
but she has never known
this black grief
of child death.

This hell,
        our hell,
is hard to bear.

Celebrate

We've been wandering
the streets of this city
for two hours now,
looking for that tiny place
my father loved so much
for its greasy enchiladas
and corn-and-peas rice
and runny refried beans.
Sweat slides
down my back,
despite the wind bursts
thrashing my hair
and turning power lines
like great black jump ropes
suspended in blue.
My feet have roused flames
inside my
not-for-walking-three-miles shoes,
my heart bangs harsh
against my head
and my eyes blink grit
every other second.

If my father were here,
he would know exactly
where we'd gone wrong.

Fiery reds and lime greens
and sunrise oranges

trade their bright
for the drab gray
of office buildings.
The boys stop and turn.
Jerry shrugs, his face an apology.

*Maybe we should
just eat here,* he says.
He rubs an eye.

That place is important to him
because his grandfather remains
inside its graffiti walls,
all those neon purple stones
stacked like memory rocks.
Losing him, losing her,
losing all these months
of our existence
to the callous of death
has been hard on us all,
but Jerry, well,
he mourns like the first grandson,
like the first brother
to cradle her pink newness
in trembling arms,
like the last brother
to pull her chilly white
to his chest.

*Why don't I go
ask for directions?* Lily says.
Before any of us can answer,

she's already disappeared
through red wood doors.
My eyes lift to your face.
This kind of questioning,
this asking another restaurant
where the competition is located,
makes you uncomfortable,
but she has never been like you,
never thought like you,
even if she was born
the same day.

We wait, watching
concrete-bound wood posts
wave and shift in the sky.

Lily appears and points
down a street we haven't walked,
only circled around.
That way, she says,
and we follow.

I stumble on uneven concrete.
Your hand steadies me,
your eyes grazing my face,
and because I don't return that gaze,
because I stare instead
at the arch dangling above us
and the field stretching beside us
and the train station looming
in front of us,
a realization creeps cold

toward my heart.
Here is where I met
the other woman,
on a night not so long ago.

And suddenly it's all
just too much,
the walking
and the embittering
and the slow, agonizing dying.
The sun dims in tiny splotches
and then larger ones
until nothing remains
to be seen
or heard
or felt.

Your arms are lifting me
from cement and old glass
and dirt-rocks
when the light returns in pinpricks.
Like the slow stir
from a vision-filled sleep,
I notice your face
and then their faces,
everyone turned toward me,
wrapped up in man arms.
One of my hands
is scraped and sore,
but still I try to push
from your hold.
You just grip tighter,

and then you kiss me,
a long kiss bursting with words
and anguish and need,
and I can do nothing
but yield.

The eyes have looked ahead
by the time that kiss softens
and you set me
on my feet again.
After a clumsy silence,
Lily points again.
There, she says,
and the boys trail her once more.
You stay, your eyes
burning questions.

But we have not come here
for this today.

We have come here
to celebrate Jerry,
to mark his eighteen years of life
with greasy enchiladas
and corn-and-peas rice
and mushy refried beans.
We have come
to feel those purple stones of memory,
to brush our hands
against their cool smooth
and remember the man
who lives within them still.

We have come
to begin our living
without her.

I don't know
how to celebrate
my son's birthday
one week after
my daughter's death.
But I will try.

I turn away from you
and follow their line
into a white-faced bistro,
your steps clicking
on pavement behind me.

Room

I wake to a
hushed house.

The boys have returned
for their last week of school.
You are probably downstairs,
holed up in your office
where you've been
composing again.
I am wrapped
in tangled sheets.

I wrench myself
from the knots
and pull a jacket
over my shoulders.
The bedroom door rasps
like the drug-worn voice
of my mother.
I step down a
morning-gray hallway,
my bare feet
marking a path
that is no longer familiar
to this dusty wood floor.
Her door stands stiff and cold,
as if expecting me today.
I close my eyes,
my hand on silver.

Maya wings across my vision,
black hair trailing,
blueberry eyes crinkling,
no-teeth-missing-yet smile
glowing the dark.
She beckons with
too-small fingers
that brush my face,
and they feel like wet tears
slipping to my chin
and my neck
and all the way to my heart.

I turn the knob
and step into a place
so full of her
I can scarcely breathe.

I haven't been in this room
since the day she left us.
A lacy curtain covers the window,
barring warmth and light and possibility.
Her favorite stuffed wolf,
gray coat matted,
stares up at an open closet
like he expects her hands
to lift him and press him close
and carry him where
she has gone.
Some clothes,
the last clothes she wore
before wiggling into that swimsuit,

lie on the floor
just in front of the
mural we painted.

My heart twists.
I would give anything
in the world
to see her
in those clothes again.

I slip beneath her covers
and the blanket I made
for her first birthday,
breathing deep the coconut
and lemon and traces of lavender
confined in those fibers.
I close my eyes,
memories flicking across the black
like scenes in a movie,
her new fist raised and pink
against the bright-white hospital walls,
her four-toothed smile
when she found her legs,
her smooth hand reaching
into my father's ashes
to grant his freedom.
My eyes burn wet.

The door shifts,
and someone enters,
but I do not turn,
only curl into a tighter ball.

A hand touches my face,
and a voice reaches
the raw of my heart.

It won't always be this way,
Lily says, and my eyes
sweep her face,
so like yours
and so like Maya's,
and I wonder how she can say
something like this
when the sting of death
has not yet faded.
And maybe she feels
the question there between us
because she sags on that bed,
and she rubs her face
and she whispers,
I have known this hell,
and I know those words for truth
because of the ghosts
lining her face
and the scars
shadowing her eyes.

　　She tells me then
of a son we never knew existed,
a son who might have been born
just after Sean and Ray
if he hadn't died
in her womb.
　　She tells me

of the years after and a daughter
who almost made it
and another who did make it,
only to die ten days later.
She tells me of a hell
where we kept them coming
and she kept them dying.

We're both weeping
by the time her voice
shudders into silence.

How in this cruelest of worlds
can one be expected
to live again?

Understanding unfolds
like the feather shield
of a mother's wing
after a too-violent storm.
This is why she has come,
to live again,
to help us live again,
and I know that her coming
is as much for her
as it is for us.

I wrap my arms around her
and hope my embrace
will speak the words
I cannot find.

Stay here forever
if that's what you need.

Wishing

My dreams,
when I find sleep,
brim with all
that I lack,
with all that is Maya
and the one before her,
with all that is
a daughter.

This wishing to change the past
is like trying to steer steady
while staring
in a rearview mirror.

I know this
because when I was young,
I spent too many
moments wishing.

     Wishing
my mother
were different,
that she did not have blue
and yellow
and needle-holed arms,
that she would not bring
       violent
       vagrant
       not-quite-sober

                men
into our home,
that she could have found it in her
to stay awake to the world
just long enough
to hear my graduation speech.

        Wishing
my father
were involved,
that he would bring with him
            order and stability
a little dad-warmth to our home
like the other fathers I knew,
that he could somehow
save her from herself,
that he might just
come around at all.

        Wishing
I were normal
like all the other kids.

                Wishing never
                changed a thing
                for me.

Still, today, I feel
that old wishing
sliding in.
Here I am,
sitting in the waiting room

of a doctor's office,
trying to read a book
I carry with me
to all the places
that remind me of her,
        which is everywhere.
A mother is talking on a phone.
I try not to listen,
but her voice crowds
the words I'm reading,
and after a moment,
I give up.
She is talking
to her daughter, I think,
asking her about the babies,
listening to the answer
that chimes faintly
from the phone.
Her face pinches a little,
and her voice
holds soft sympathy
when she speaks again.
I'm so sorry
I can't be there.
It will be OK, sweetie.

And then that
        wishing
begins to burn its hole
in my chest
and prick its needles
in my eyes

and smudge its great black marker
across the pencil-line of recovery
so my focus blurs and shifts
and slips toward remember.

I wanted that,
in my aging.
A daughter friend.
I wanted someone
who would call
        for advice
        to share funny stories
                about grandchildren
        just to talk.
I wanted that,
and the wishing gnaws
its way to the hollow
of my deep.

Memories
        good and bad
and all those in between
flick across my vision.
By the time they fade,
a weary ache
coats my bones.

I will never know the gift
of a forever friend
with raven hair
and blueberry eyes
and porcelain-doll skin.

The tears begin their torrent
right there in that waiting room,
where stranger's eyes find my face
and then books on laps,
and they don't dry up
even after I've
somehow made
my way home
and somehow
unlocked the front door
and somehow
fumbled up the stairs
and into her room
and beneath the covers of her bed.
I pull them over my face
to black out the world,
to stop the tear torrent,
to welcome the dreams
that brim with all I lack.

When I wake,
Leo's hand warms my arm
and Jerry's arm has slipped
beneath my neck
and Chris's fingers wrap my ankle.
Sean and Ray kneel beside the bed,
their elbows resting
just beside me.
You stand in the doorway,
glowing in fading twilight,
your gaze moving

from boy to boy to me.

We breathe and resolve
and grow stronger
in this moment together,
seven strands
in a cord not easily broken.
The force of our connection speaks,
and I hear the words
we could never, ever say aloud,
words we know and understand
in only our secret places.

We will look back no longer.

Best

The finality of the grave
could not silence
your father.

He was a bully
through and through,
and he speaks even today,
after all these years.
His voice sneaks up on me
when I'm tending
the flowers in my garden.
You'll never be able
to fix her to rights.
When I'm painting
in my sun room,
shapes curling color
on white canvas.
What kind of dream is that?
When I'm scrubbing dishes
or folding laundry
or stirring soup.
She'll never make you happy.

Your father
never saw
the good in me.

We walk this stone path
unfolding through a field

where marble markers
jut from the earth
like thousands of white-gray hands
raised in remembrance.
The names,
etched on these stones,
tell of courage and power
and anguish.
Not all of them came home
like your father did.

His stone lies in the back.
He is an old man
resting among the young.
Flags crackle in the wind,
the gift of some
dedicated soul
who couldn't bear
that these men
be forgotten on their
honor day.

Lily carries a clay pot
with the three daisies
Leo carefully unearthed
from his flower garden
and repotted
so your father's burial place
might glow with
color and beauty.
As we near the headstone,
he hands the pot to Lily.

Her knees touch the ground
where your father was lowered
that rainy afternoon
seven years ago.
She did not bid him farewell then,
too caught up in her own pain,
in her own burying of babies
to fly home.
I know that now,
though I didn't then.

Today is her farewell.

So we have come here,
bearing the fire of the sun,
to remember
the white-whiskered man
with a voice
      hoarse
      and harsh
      and sharp
        as a metal-tipped whip,
at least when it
faced my direction.

He was a good man, Lily says,
and I wonder about
this man she knew
and why he was not
the same one I knew,
the one who disowned his son
because of an unapproved marriage,

the one who never knew
his grandsons
because he needed
to make his point,
the one who withheld
what could easily
have been given
right up until the hour
he died.

You move forward,
sweat gleaming on your forehead,
and kneel beside your sister.
She takes your hand
and leans her head
on your shoulder.

He was a hard man, you say,
and I shift, feeling like a spectator
listening in on something
not meant for me.
I turn toward the boys,
who have moved off
to read the words
on other gravestones.
Your father's marble
is just one in a million
to them.

No harder than most, Lily says.
He only wanted what was best for us.
I try not to taste the bitter

that climbs my throat.
He just didn't always
know what that best was.

I watch the flags bending
and coiling in the wind.
Your sister twists back then,
her eyes finding mine.
Help me plant it? she says,
raising the pot of daisies.

Our sleeves brush
in the trading places
and then I'm kneeling
and you're standing
and Lily's digging with bare hands
and a spade Leo brought.
When the hole gapes deep enough
and we finally move
the three flowers
to its earth hollow,
dirt coats our hands
and our knees
and the skin beneath our fingernails.
We sit back on our heels,
where we can better see
the orange petals
gleaming against the gray.

He just didn't always
know what was best for us, Lily says then,
and her eyes invite me

into her knowing,
into her forgiving,
into her loving.
Her hand pats my leg,
silent words tapping strength
and conviction
and truth
to the very deep of me.

I was the best.
Your father didn't know this,
but Lily did
and you did
and I do, now, today.

Your eyes are shining
when we turn
and follow stone steps
and flailing flags
and marble markers
back toward home.

True or False

The air hangs thick and sultry
as I pace toward
my father's park.
Maya was my company
after he died.
Today I walk this path
wholly alone
but for the memories:
the shuffle of his limp-step
and her skip-step,
the warm of his elbow
in my hand
and her fingers weaving mine.

A bench, red paint chipping,
lies just ahead,
one we always used to pass
because of the other ones
in the squared center of green
where my father's friends
used to sleep and assemble
and wait for good conversation.
This foreign one
will hold me today.
Birds screech and lift
as I sink into its cool,
disturbed from their
cracker-crumb feast.

The park is near empty.
On the fringes,
some of my father's friends
rest in shade,
their grimy faces turned
from those who might look too long.
I stare at beckoning trees,
at thirsty grass,
at a bright red ball
that bounces its end
just inches from my foot.

It's the sort of treasure
that would have
caught Maya's eye,
and this is why I pick it up
and this is why I roll it
between my fingers
and this is why I search
the perimeter for its owner.

A child, a tiny little girl,
lurches toward me,
her hands lifted in front of her.
I bend and hold the ball out,
but she doesn't notice.
Ball, she says, and her grin
is a great, wide, shining sun.
She stops, bending
to touch the grass,
her hands patting earth.
She stands again, marching on.

Here's your ball, I say then.
The red of it glows in the sun rays
glaring through tree leaves.
Her head twists toward me,
and that's when I see them,
those blueberry eyes
that belonged to Maya,
those eyes that rove
toward and past and through,
those eyes that cannot see.

Ball, she says when I close it
in her hand. Her laugh
chimes and floats and swells
in a magical melody
that binds us in hope.

Yes, I say, and she throws it again,
this time past my feet,
so I have to stop its bounce.
I press it once more
into her tiny hand.
She laughs and I smile
and the deep inside
begins its great thaw.

We play together,
the two of us,
one who sees
every bounce of that ball
and one who will never know

the color red,
until a woman on another bench
calls out a word,
one I don't understand,
in a raspy voice I do understand,
and the child's smile dims
and her blueberry eyes widen
and her legs,
purple-pocked and ash-scarred,
propel her back
toward the woman.
I see red on her thighs
where the diaper
has rubbed skin raw,
and the burden of knowing
tears at my shoulders
because I can do nothing
without a name
or an address
or some information bit
to feed authorities.

The woman, gaunt and pale,
swings the girl
onto a bony hip
and strides toward the street.
Just once the child
looks back my way
with eyes that see nothing
but feel everything.
And when she does,
I remember.

This is the child I saw
the day of Maya's funeral,
the day of my too-long walk,
the day I watched her stumble
into a house chipped and leaning,
into a world that plays
with fire and ice
and kerosene jugs
sitting too close
to gaping doorways.

By the time I stand to leave,
the sun has begun its slumber
and the girl's face
has become Maya's
and I don't know
if what I have seen
is true or false.

Miles

The sky bleeds fire
by the time you pull the door
closed behind you
and we climb
to the top of our street and
        stretch our stride
        fall into step
        match our breath.

Something sacred
and noble and magnificent
exists in this inhaling of love
and trust and everything
that is good,
in this exhaling of hatred
and doubt and all
that is shadow-dark.

Something familiar
exists in this
foot cadence.

Here is where we began,
all those years ago.

I fall a step behind you,
the way I always have
because you,
in your quietly competitive way,

prefer to be inches ahead,
and the first time
I tried to keep perfect pace,
we ended that run
with too-red faces
and too-laboring lungs
and too-blazing thighs.

The sky grows dark
and dull and moon-less
while we breathe and breathe
and keep on breathing.
I glance ahead,
where light reaches
its spotted yellow arms
toward gray.
I glance behind,
where trees huddle
around the life within.
I glance beside,
where you fix
your gaze on what
I cannot see.

What secrets
move in your mind
when you run?

Maybe you've shared.
Maybe you've kept.
Maybe you would like
to ask the same of me.

And because I know
that some secrets loiter
and grow and melt away
the very best parts of a heart,
I will tell you:
I think on leaving
and on staying
and on you.

So it is that after nine miles
of shared step and breath and pace,
I know you better
than I did when the sky
held fire instead of ink.
I know you never intended
to do what you did.
I know you grieve
       because of it
       because of her
       because of me
         and my not-knowing.

I know you wait
              because you love.

And when we
shorten our strides
and slow our breath
and begin to walk
with shuddering legs,
I know something more

that maybe I have
known all along.

I will stay
because I love.

Lead

Pool balls click
one against another,
tapping into pockets,
thumping against the wood sides,
cracking against your sticks.
You and your best friend
walk the table,
straight-backed and sure,
like it hasn't been fifteen years
since you last played this game.
You pretend,
the both of you,
to know what you're doing,
but I know better.
You're just lucky.

A woman, leaning her back
against a table
seating two others,
stares at you from her place,
dark makeup-smudged eyes
roving the length of you.
I look too, surprised by the
gentle warm that stirs my deep.
These weeks and their long runs
away from the home pain
and their heavy weights
to divert the sorrow weights
have chiseled and transformed.

You look younger
than your years now,
even with tragedy's scars
puckering your eyes.

You and Brad laugh
about something,
but I am not close enough to hear.
Your face glows
in the smoke shadows.
You pat his back,
and he glances my way.
I stir my drink,
studying the salted rim
so I only feel your eyes
on my face.

When I lift my gaze again,
the short-skirted staring woman
is between the two of you,
leaning your way.
She says something to you,
her mouth close to your ear,
her hand resting on your chest,
and the jealousy rolls toward me,
      violent
      alarming
      unexpected
like the black clouds that carry
summer's wildest storms.

I will not do this again.

I turn away,
dousing lightning sparks
with another drink.
I taste angry and bitter
and terrified
in that long and fiery swallow.

A hand grips my shoulder
and pulls me around.

Dance with me, you say.

I shake my head.
We're not dancers, I say.

Dance with me,
you say again,
like you haven't heard,
and this time you don't wait
for my no,
just draw me to my feet
and press me tight to your chest
and fit my arms
around your shoulders
and my face
into your neck fold.
Your arms, strong
and tender and immovable,
tell me what
your mouth doesn't.

I am yours.

And somewhere in the middle
of that song,
love cuts in
and slides all the way down,
and by the time
the music fades,
tears wash my cheeks
of the smoke
and the grime
and the kisses you drop
beside my lip
and on my eye corner
and in that cherish-place
above my brows.

Let's go home, I say,
and you lead the way
out the door.

Dance

A night-dark room,
     a whispered song,
          one more dance
to the melody unspoken.

We touch
     breathe
          turn together,
move together

reach together
     toward the light that promises
          to shatter black   distance
all that has come before.

And when we have reached it
     passed through it
          come to rest
on its other side

when we have joined
     our tears
          our words
our love

when we have become,
     together,
          what we could not
be alone

I know that
        we have turned a page
                with the same hand
and we have read

what is written
        with the same eyes
                and we have understood it all
with the same throbbing heart.

I slide into sleep
        with your legs tangled in mine
                your arm heavy across my chest
your body pressed warm

against my back.

Sit

Music vibrates
in the distance,
muffled throbs that
       shake my chest
       thump my head
       beat my heart.
An airplane growls
just overhead,
full of those on their way
to vacation liberty
and those returning
to re-entry shock.

The boys turn burgers
on a park grill.
You watch them from a distance,
and I watch you.
A white bird darts toward blue,
wings flapping
in hasty retreat
from the steps of some children
who race past.
It perches in the tree above me,
waiting for the feast
it hopes to glean
from our crumbs.

I stare at the fruit cup
in my hand, full of

watermelon soaking up
the tart of pineapple,
strawberry lending its sweet
to cantaloupe,
grapes wearing colors
that are not their own,
sealing holes
that the other morsels
could not fill.

Our love-lives together
are a lot like that fruit.
We bleed our colors
and soak up flavors
and hues not our own
and seal the yawning holes
in the deep down
so we are made richer
for the sharing.

You and I.
Us and them.
Her and us.

The water beside me
is cloudy green,
like something has churned
so long beneath its shallow depths
that it has forgotten
the clear glass it used to be.
It shifts in the barely-there breeze,
rippling memories groping for me.

I feel my own water
block my throat
and sting my eyes.
She always loved this place
with its river water
and duck friends.

Something shifts
on the edge of my sight,
and I see Jerry
staring at the water, too.
His eyes shine with
regret and missing
and might have been.
In those murky waters,
he sees her,
the little girl he'd held,
the very day she was born,
in eleven-year-old
big brother arms,
the little girl he'd
promised to protect
from that beginning,
the little girl he
could not save.

I see him again,
curling over her,
pumping and breathing
and listening again and again and again,
until the men leapt
from their rescue cars,

until four of them
dragged him away from her body,
until his guttural howl
covered all of our wails.

Will he never
love water again?

He wipes at his face,
and I don't even feel myself
begin to move,
but I do,
and when I've reached him,
my breath comes in gasps
so I can't speak,
just wrap him up tight and hard.
He is taller than me now,
     almost a man,
but I pull him close
all the same.
He shudders and sobs and sags.

I miss her, he says
in a voice thick and wet.

I know, I say.
I stroke his hair
and kiss his head.
My eyes spill a river down my face,
and his pain chokes
and splutters and masks
the sudden smack

of skin on water.

And because his colors
have become my own,
because his seventeen years
have begun to bleed
into my forty-three,
I pull away
and touch his chin
and lift his eyes to my own.

It wasn't your fault, I say.

He crumples then,
and I am not strong enough
to hold him.
We collapse to the ground,
and then the cries and screams
and panic-shouts grab us
by the throat so we find
our feet racing toward water.
A crowd has collected, pointing.
Jerry launches into the water.

He breaks the surface
one time,
two times,
three times.
Desperation mars his face.
Your hand warms my shoulder,
and I know you know.

He is searching for her
in that murky river.

When he next breaks the surface,
he is carrying a
white-haired child, a boy,
choking and alive.
A man pulls the boy to safety,
then extends a hand to Jerry.
The crowd murmurs,
and the man,
soaked from desperation's attempt,
hugs our son and then the boy
and then our son again,
and only when the crowd
has scattered does he move
on his way,
back toward banners
and relief-tears
and mother-arms,
back to one more birthday
they all get to celebrate.

Jerry turns away from the water,
then abruptly sits on its bank.
His brothers crowd around him
in silent awe.
You pull me down next to you,
circling all of them.

We sit there for a long time,
bleeding and

soaking up and
sealing the yawning holes
in the deep down
so we are made richer
for the sharing.

Wait

This city
has many faces.

There is early morning,
when the great orange of new
stretches long fingers
to history's wood and
brick and stone,
painting the empty beautiful,
marking warm the way
toward productivity.
The city blinks awake then,
rising and swelling
and waiting with expectation
for what is to come.

There is the middle morning,
when the wind holds signs
and flags and awnings,
beating them hard
against wood and brick and stone
so the respectable,
the ones who disappear
into all that wood
and brick and stone,
can pretend they haven't heard
the hope-filled questions
of my father's friends,
who spend their morning

raiding trash cans
for the remains
of greasy breakfast food
tossed there by the respectable.
The city settles then,
crawling and hollowing
and searching for something
to ease the belly-ache.

There is midday,
when the sun grins down
on all the respectable
spilling from their
comfortable buildings
out into an
uncomfortable street,
hunting for that
perfect place to eat
and drink and be a little merry
for this one hour of reprieve.
The city heaves then,
spitting out, rolling up
and inviting back in
to the invisible.

There is middle afternoon,
when all the respectable
glance at their wristwatches
and up toward their office clocks
and out to the empty-still street,
waiting for the last tick
like a discharge button

that will thrust them, finally, home.
The city holds its breath then,
anticipating life,
awaiting release,
standing just beside
the door of freedom.

There is the hour
of too many cars,
when the air chokes
and coughs and splutters
and the friends of my father
watch all the respectable,
who don't know this city
the way they,
        the almost-forgotten,
do, drive back out
to their houses
in the suburbs, with only
the full-of-food-wrappers trash cans
and finger smudges on windows
and car exhaust smog
to tell they've been
here at all.
The city is uncompromising then,
pushing and fighting
and forgetting.

There is evening,
when the sky begins
its slow-fade and the artists
and musicians and lovers

step from behind
their respectable masks
and the lights burn
like artificial stars,
red and blue
and every single shade
of yellow.
The city feels alive then,
rolling and winking
and beckoning.

There is midnight,
when the lights flicker out,
when my father's friends
stretch their lithe forms
across the wood of benches,
when the sky flaunts its glitter,
one here, one there,
just a few bright enough
to see in urban glow.
The city sleeps then,
dreaming and hoping
and envisioning
something better.

Our lives are like this city
with its many faces.

My life alone:
middle morning.

My life with the boys:

early morning.

My life with you:
middle afternoon.

We wait, holding our breath,
anticipating life,
standing just beside
the door of freedom.

Places

Gravel coils in front of me,
tiny rocks grinding
beneath my feet,
but no matter how
keenly I listen,
I cannot hear her steps.
The trees, lending shade
from a flaming sun,
bend and beckon,
but no matter how
carefully I look,
I cannot see her form
hiding behind
the largest of them.
The wind sighs
hot breath in my face,
but no matter how
much of it I feel,
the touch of her hand
eludes me.

This is a place she loved,
every week,
every season.
This is a place I loved,
with her.

Love it I can do
no longer.

I walk the trails,
the places
where we would stop
to examine a praying mantis,
green and stooped,
where we would stuff
our treasure-rocks
in bulging pockets,
where we would sit,
her feet swinging,
to craft our stories
about the people passing us by.

Summer oppression
traces its fingers
down the small of my back
and pools its wet
at the base of my neck
and dampens the skin
above my lip.
The grass sags,
brown and tired of this
beating-down sun.

My letting go
is a lot like this
summer drought,
boiling and stifling
and too, too hard to bear.
I am like that grass,
wilting, then rising,

then wilting again
until I brown and curl
and die day by day,
week by week,
month by month.

Relief, like her hand,
eludes me today.

I walk and walk
and keep on walking
until I have passed those doors,
        the ones we used to
        race inside, three times,
until the heat and tears
and memories have choked
the air from me,
until I know I must cross
that entry in this,
the last of our
sacred sharing places.

So I do, cool air rippling
across my skin-damp.
The butterflies that drew her
to their corner wait for one
who will never call again.
They do not twirl and dance
and fly on their
invisible strings today
because I do not breathe
and she does not laugh.

Rows and rows of books,
the couch where we'd hunch
over our borrowed reads,
an encyclopedia,
the same one she chose
to bring home a dozen times,
turned toward me
on the floor,
and then the heat slips inside
these fortressed walls, too,
and I cannot be here
without her.

How will I ever be here
without her?

My eyes sting
as I turn toward the door
and blaze
as I walk toward my car
but spill
only after I sit behind the wheel.

This, the last
of our sacred sharing places.
I swallow my goodbye,
roll the ignition
and steer down the winding path
where you and the boys
and a life I have yet
to live awaits.

Living

This is what I remember.

A red glare, unexpected,
cloaking the cars ahead,
a warm swell of panic
sweeping my face
and chest and toes,
a foot thrusting,
too late.

The crunch-rub of
metal against metal,
the windshield spiders climbing,
widening, caving
so sharp knives scream
toward my belted body.

Then a voice,
a man shouting,
strong hands jerking,
lights flashing
and exploding and now
fading as the black
swallows all.

This is all I remember.

I don't remember living.

Words

Light beams through the
shade-screened window,
reaching thick fingers
toward carpet,
a row of chairs,
my blue-blanketed leg.
You sit hunched in a seat,
your skin burning
golden with sun.
Your shoulders slump,
just like the shoulders
of your sons,
who join your edge,
like a defense-line,
in the back of this strange
yet too-familiar room.

Then you notice my staring,
and you rise on silently swift feet
and stand tall at my bedside.
Your hand grips mine.

I don't understand, I say
because all I remember
are those butterflies
and that red glare of cars
and a spidering windshield.

An accident, you say.

Jerry's hand strokes my hair
and Leo's hand fits my other hand
and Chris moves beside you,
his fingers curling my arm,
and Sean and Ray square me in
at the foot of this bed.
Wires bind the hand you grip
to a machine beside you.

Twelve eyes rub my face,
all of them leaking water
and worry and the agony of me,
trapped in this bed.

We got the call, you say,
like you owe me an explanation
for all the wet,
but your voice cracks
in the middle of that word,
and you sob your terror
away from me,
toward the neon
of the uncaring machine
that marks every beat
of my heart
and measures
every lung-breath.
Chris strokes your back,
his filling-again eyes
dropping to my arm.

An accident, I say

with a thick-from-sleep tongue,
and it's only then
that my body begins its ache,
like a noiseless storm of black
thundering its injurious way
from my chest
to the toes tenting
the bottom of my covers.

*Some bones broken
in your leg,* Leo says.

Some glass cuts, Jerry says,
pointing to my chest.
I lower my eyes to the
dotted hospital gown.
A bandage peeks white
from the top.

The windshield, you say,
and I see again
the magnificent explosion,
all that glass
stinging me in fury.
Your eyes, red-rimmed
and swollen, rest on mine again.

I nod. *How long?* I say.

Two days, Sean says,
his voice tight.
Ray's hand on my foot twitches,

almost imperceptibly,
and I know,
in my deep down,
what this waiting has done to them,
what it will continue doing to them
until I am safe at home.

My eyes drag open
past heaviness,
sleep, a knowing
conspirator in healing,
fighting me,
a reluctant-to-leave-them-
so-soon-after-waking victim.
I study my boys,
tall posts beside this bed,
and you, wrecked beside them,
and I remember the last time
we were all
gathered here, together,
in a place white
and unfeeling
and merciless
while we wept the loss
of a great treasure.

This is not a sacred sharing place,
but maybe this is the last
of her places
we had to come, together,
before we could wrestle
our way forward.

I'm OK, I say,
my voice smeared broad
with fatigue.
The boys lean in
to kiss my cheek,
one at a time.
Jerry lingers longer,
squeezing my hand in his.
I'm OK, I say again
because his eyes
are fear-shadows,
even still.

He nods, his eyes
like black glass,
and files from the room
behind his brothers.
Only you remain.

You rest your head on mine.
I thought I'd lost you, you say.

There was a time,
not so very long ago,
when I thought the same
of you.

My hand rises to your cheek,
pain stabbing my chest.

I'm still here, I say,

and your tears wash my forehead.

You unbend again,
a tower of strength
in this room of white weakness,
tethering me to the ground,
to life, to the five of them
waiting just outside the door.

And then words
I never thought to hear
from you again,
rising from the night
like a morning-glow tower
of their own.

I love you.

Truth

Words have their way
of sliding way down
to that place of mystery,
that place of essence,
that cindery cage of self,
and awakening the truth
from its hiding place.

And all these words
crowding the white mummy-cloth
wrapping my leg,
      so much like
      that old bench
      where you squeezed in
      your love-declaration
      onto those wooden planks
      while I sipped red soda
      and dreamed about
      what married would look like,
hoist up that truth
      fling it out
          stir it into a flame-ocean
that soaks and singes
and boils all at the
same time.

Lily,
words that thank me
for understanding

her need to be here,
         with us,
for a time.
Sean, a word-puzzle
that speaks of love and hope.
Ray, a word-poem
that sings my beauty and care.

Jerry: *I love you
more than you could
ever know, Mom,*
and I think how I do know
the grand of this love,
only magnified.

Leo: *You water my soul,*
and I wonder how
this boy, so young,
can understand the mystery
that is love.

Chris: *Painting you
a flower, Mom,
because this is what
you are in my life,*
and I think that maybe
they all value
more than I
let myself see.

And then these from you:
That scar on your heart

just proves you have
given yourself in love,
fully and completely.
Thank you for loving
me and the boys so well.
I vow today and always
to love you well, too.
I wonder if
      this newborn awareness
      this abiding love
      this restored promise
are disaster's secret beauties.

You've all gathered
in this room again
because today is my
going home day,
and we have all been
waiting for this freedom.
The surgical scar
just beside my heart
itches now,
healing from the inside out,
and though it is raised
and gnarled and it
splits my chest
in a finger-long line,
none of that matters now
from where I sit,
waiting for the crutches
that will walk me
toward home.

Jerry hands them to me.
I pull myself up,
his hand on my arm,
and set them
beneath my shoulders.

Let's go home, you say,
your hand on my back.
You all share a smile
before we begin our
shuffle-and-limp dance
out that windowless door.

Hook

The way out
of the hospital
is a maze of
dim corridors
and emergency exits.

Almost there, you say
when I stop for a rest.
The crutches have rubbed
my underarms raw.
*We should have gotten
you a wheelchair.*

*Need us to carry you
the rest of the way?* Jerry says,
his eyes laughing.

I smile and hobble
forward in answer.
The automatic doors slide open,
and the air puffs
angry heat in my face.
Your hand steadies me,
pressed flat to my back.

I'll get the car, you say
when I've limped across
the metal thresholds,
and Leo takes your place beside me,

lowering me down
to a bench.
My leg pulses
its rhythm of pain.
The boys stand guard around me,
the wind stinging our eyes
with dirt and fire.

The engine of a car,
idling on the edge
of this pick-up circle,
shudders into speed-up,
and the ancient vehicle
lurches forward.
At exactly the same moment,
the automatic doors swish open,
expelling cool air to
stroke our backs,
and a little girl waddles
from behind their safety, alone,
headed straight
for the car-path.

Jerry moves
before I can blink
or think or help-shout,
launching toward the girl
on feet that never once
touch the cement.
He lifts her
just before the car
staggers through,

its antique driver
unaware of anything amiss.

A man, thin and haggard,
his cigarette still clenched
between yellow teeth,
ends his sprint
just outside those doors.
Jerry clutches the girl
to his chest.
One of her hands
rests on the back of his neck.
The other pats his face.
The beach-sunset postcard
she carried before Jerry's rescue
stares from the ground
for a split moment
before the wind
peels it from gray
and lifts it toward blue.

The girl turns,
her hands still tiny
on Jerry's neck and face.
Those blueberry eyes
see nothing.
My eyes blur.

The man, the one she calls Dada,
steps forward, mumbling his thanks
and pulling the girl from stranger arms.
We watch him stalk back inside,

his voice raised harsh and hostile,
his hand smacking
her purple-pocked leg
in three quick hits.

The doors close behind them,
but their glass can't
quiet her scream.

I look at Jerry,
the hero once again,
but when his eyes
finally tear away
from the girl and her father
and touch mine,
I know that he feels
nothing like a hero.
The memory of her,
the one he could not save,
is still caught on his skin
like a sneering, empty hook.

His eyes leak and pour
long after you shift your stop
in front of us,
long after the boys tell you
of his heroics,
long after you wordlessly
help me to my seat
and crawl toward
the circle's end.

Gift

The summer evening is warm,
cicadas clicking and humming
in a great disharmony
as we twist our way
home from the hospital.
Wind-breath puffs in my face
and through my hair
and into the backseat,
where a wordless Jerry
stares out the window,
away from her old seat.
Your hand strokes
the back of my neck.
The other boys
whisper in back seats,
and Leo's laugh
dances with the wind.

My leg thumps pain,
every stop and turn
and bump a silent
agony to me.

You drive slowly, warily,
like the way we crawled
that road home
with a brand-new Jerry,
you in the front,
me in the back,

my arms spread protectively
around the buckled-tight seat
where he slept.
You drive like I am
that same costly cargo,
and the burn of my leg
walks up to my heart
and settles deep.

The warm of wind
and the stroke of hand
and the gentle drone
of all these voices,
man and boy and insect,
drag my eyelids
toward my leg,
and before I even know
what's happened,
your face has shifted
to my other side,
and you say, *We're home.*
You pull me gently
from my seat.

The boys wait
outside the car,
all eyes on me.
Color, strange
and unfamiliar here,
swims in my eye-corner,
so I turn my head
to the house.

And there, against its side,
is Maya.

I know her even though
the eyes glow too blue
and the hair gleams too brown.
I know her
because of the butterfly
so like the ones
she tried to catch
and the color gems
so like those sharp rocks
she collected and painted
and the flowers
so like the swirl-circles
she used to draw.

Welcome home, the six of you say,
man voices blending with boy.

My eyes smear and spill
with this gift.
You lift me to your chest.

The eyes aren't right, Chris says,
his eyes on the ground.
And the hair.
I couldn't get
the colors right.

It's beautiful, I say,

my voice rough and tight.

You hold me there,
with you and the boys
and Maya painted on the house,
until light shifts to shadow,
and then we walk,
all of us in step together,
toward the front door.

Vacancy

Vacancy lives here,
in these spaces between words,
in these pauses before wake,
in all this dark
connecting all this light.

Here, too, lives
break and heal.

In the days
after my hospital stay,
Lily brings breakfast
to my bedside table
and you set lunch there
four hours later
and we gather for dinner
at a dining table filled with food
cooked by the boys.
The seven of you
tend me like a priceless jewel,
and this leaves me
nothing to do
but think.

My mind,
like a ring going forth
and circling round,
huddles in this vacancy,
in all those

        spaces
        pauses
        uneven shadows
thinking of her
        thinking of us
                thinking of what
comes next.

Here in this home,
surrounded by all of you,
I move slowly
toward that repair place,
but it is not
an alone-moving.
We all press onward
into that silence between steps,
in and out of these
days turned night,
through the deserts
of our deeps.

And yet there is still this,
filling all the vacancy:
love that binds wounds.

The globes of this love
glow vivid at the bottom
of the dark.
You. The boys.
Lily.

And there between them all,

living in her own bottom-dark,
is a little girl, nameless,
with violet eyes
that cannot see bright
but can surely give it.

This little girl
visits my vacancy,
that yawning empty between
words and silence,
wake and sleep,
day and night,
and her filling lends
its own blue-glow
to the dark of
who I have been
and who I really am
and who I could
possibly be.

Hope takes up
its wordless tune
in a scar-marked deep
that has known too much
vacancy.

New

The trees just
outside her window
bend in a wind invisible,
a breath of newness shaking
leaves to the ground,
clearing the way for change.
Fall hides in that wind,
behind all those trees,
inside a beating-down sun.

Newness glints
in my breast, too,
a candle bud
snuffed to almost
blue nothing.

I turn from the window
and back to her room,
empty with silence
yet packed with sound,
all those memories
reeling like an
eye-screen movie:
her tiny pink form that first day,
her laugh-light that first year,
her crooked smile just yesterday.

I stand in the room center,
     remembering

yearning
        studying.
That bed, the blanket
I made her last year
covering its top.
That table with the
sewing machine,
where she crafted
a crooked pillow for you.
That wall with the
bulletin board, tacked tight
with her drawings.

A microphone stand
catches my eye
in the windowed corner.
She put it there
after Chris drew that wall mural
because she said his creativity
made her more creative,
and she wanted to stare at it
while composing.
I touch the cold plastic,
remembering her delight
when you brought that gift home,
remembering the first song
she wrote for you,
remembering the endless week
of capturing her family's
voices on its record roll.

And then a child's voice

melts into the walls,
into the very frame
of this house where
she is no more,
singing about Sadie,
that stuffed dog we used to
all pretend, for her,
was part of our family.
A giggle ends her song,
and a kiss, probably for Sadie,
and then there is me
in the background.
You're so silly, I say,
and this me today,
this me who has lived
too many hours and
too many days and
too many months without her,
does not think
she is silly at all,
only so beautiful
and so wonderful
and so perfect.

Her voice ruptures
the scar-flesh of my deep
and lodges its spike there.

How do I do this?
How do I get rid of this blanket
that has touched her body in sleep,
and how do I give away

this sewing machine
that bears her fingerprints still
and how do I clear out
this microphone
that holds within it
the memory of her voice,
proving she once lived after all?

How do I keep them?

Erin. Lily moves beside me,
an arm around my waist,
breaking my fall.

I can't do this, I say,
my voice liquid and tight
and heavy with this grief-burden.

You don't have to, she says,
and she moves me
toward the door.
My crutches click
their tap dance
and then Lily closes the door to
            that room
where I cannot breathe
            that room
where she used to live
            that room
where the black of sorrow
coils like a restless viper.

You stand behind us,
and when we turn,
you lift me into your arms.

Those winds
that bend the trees outside,
they are not
the breath of new after all.
New is not welcome here
yet.

Forgiven

We sit alone in our room,
the first time in all these
boy-doctor days,
and the house whispers
around us, quiet ringing
hum-notes in our ears.

I lie on the bed,
a book open in front of me.
You sit on the edge,
not too close, not too far,
like the way you approached me
back at the beginning,
vigilant and tender and uncertain.

Your eyes warm my face.
I pretend to read
until you find words.

When I got that call, you say.

I finger my bookmark,
my eyes leaving the page
and landing on you.
Your eyes melt liquid.

I thought, you say,
your voice cracking around us,
yet, in the same moment,

loosening and weakening
and then felling the walls
thick around my deep down.
I thought I had lost
another of my girls.
Your cheeks glisten drops,
your eyes cracked and clear
like the van's front window,
and I know this is not
just about that call.
So I wait. My book bends closed.

Your hand seals hard
around mine,
clenching my fingers
until yours bleed white.
I'm so sorry, you say.
I'm so sorry.
Over and over and over again
the words wriggle free
of your lips and then
shake free all that's
buried deep in the both of us.
You shudder and you shake
and you sob your great sorrow,
a sorrow much like
the losing of our daughter,
          cavernous and mysterious,
a sorrow for what
might have been.
After minutes or hours
or days even

your breath quiets,
and you speak again.
I'm sorry for hurting you.

The words push between us,
hollowing out all that hurt
and all that fear
and all that resentment
I tried to leave
at the grave of our daughter.
And then, the words
that surprise us both:

I forgive you, I say.

Your eyes lift to mine,
dripping clear again.

*I'm sorry I didn't
tell you sooner,* you say.

Forgiven, I say.

*I'm sorry I left you
with my body,* you say.

Forgiven, I say.

And after you have
said your say,
loosed all your sadness
and all those disappointments

and all the anxiety-turned despair,
and after I have torn the veil
between my bitter disillusionment,
        the disconnection that
        walled me secure,
and you,
and after we have
both of us forgiven,
we sit there together,
on the grape cover of our bed,
tethered tight by the wonder
that is forgiveness.

And when the silence
wrapping us swells and bulges
and threatens its burst,
you lift your guitar
from its peg on our wall
and begin to play a
barely-remembered melody.

Before it's over,
the boys have found their way
back into this room,
and Lily stands
in the doorway,
and then we all raise voices,
eight strong and
getting stronger,
building new walls
that are not really walls at all
for their gaping-wide doors.

Sometimes we need
this knife-wound of sorrow,
this acid-fill of mistake,
this open-wide-and-even-wider
way of healing
to press on toward greater.

Sometimes the night
is darkest just before
the rainbow-light of dawn.

Grave

The evening murmurs quiet,
all its people in other
places but this.
The sun walks
its way toward sleep
as slowly as I
limp my way
down this tree-lined path.

This day, marking Leo's
fifteenth year of life,
he chose first to come here,
to her graveside,
where a name-stone
rises from earth
like she used to stand.
My deep clenches its fist,
but we move forward,
Leo leading, me following,
you and the boys behind.

Leo carries tulips,
her favorite flower.
My crutches tick the minutes.

We stop just feet
from her grave,
where Leo stands,
a shadowing silhouette

against a fire sky
painted with goodbye.
The sun slips behind clouds,
stealing light and breath, too.
Minutes slide by,
and then I limp up
next to our son.
His tender heart shines
from his eyes.

Why today? I say.

So we can move on, he says,
and I wonder anew
at the wisdom balled up
in this boy
who has known
too much death
for his fifteen years.

He pushes forward
and kneels before
the white marble,
head bent in line
with shoulders.
The flowers smear
the grey of her stone,
like a sun rising
after the gray light of dawn.
We wait while he whispers.

And after he rises,

we wait for Chris and Ray
and Sean and finally Jerry.
You push forward then,
your hand brushing my shoulder.
I watch your bowed back
until you stand
and then you pull me forward,
lowering me to my sitting place.
You move away.

How to say goodbye
when this death,
this hole of her
that burns empty still,
is anything but good?
How to let her rest in peace
when her hole yields
nothing but turmoil
in the hearts of me
and you and them?
How to knife away
all those pieces of her
in all this whole of us?

She lives still in our home,
in the carpet fibers
where she drew
her practice letters
in permanent marker,
on that chalkboard wall
where she wrote all our names
and hers biggest of all,

in the room that holds
all her favorite books.

She lives still in them,
in the piano-fingers of Jerry
and his minor-key songs,
in the garden-hands of Leo
and all those flowers
he planted for her,
in the artist-hands of Chris
and his greatest masterpiece
there on her bedroom wall,
in the pen-hands of Ray
and all that poetry and
in the orator-voice of Sean,
her most requested reader.

She lives still
in you and me.

How does one
let go of all this?

I stare at the grave
swelling in my throat,
this lump of earth
sprouting grass once again,
this final resting place
for our beloved,
words lost and buried
down there with her.
The dark grows darker,

and then, in a last vigilant effort,
the sun escapes white
and points its glow toward me,
blinding in its brilliant blaze
before that final night-surrender,
like a fiery hope to light our path
on this way back home
from the grave.

And the words, then,
climb their way out.

I wish you could see
your picture on the side
of our house, baby.
I wish you could ring
our doorbell again.
I wish you could make a mess
in the kitchen and I could
complain about cleaning it up.

I wish we had never gone
to the pool that day.

I wish I could hear
your voice say I love you
one more time.
I wish I could feel
your arms around my neck.
I wish I could see you again
in that princess dress
you wore to your

daddy daughter dance.

I wish I could tell you
that your daddy and I
are finding our way
back to love.

I love you.
I miss you so much.
I can't do life without you,
but here I am.

And when the words
have emptied into summer wind
shaking the grass
and her flowers
and my hair,
I turn back toward
the six of you waiting for me.
You pull me up,
your eyes soft and damp.
When you kiss me,
the grief slides from my eyes,
and warm trades places
with cold there in my deep,
like a lane shifting forward.

I limp back down the path
out of this burial place,
your hand on my back,
the boys leading the way.
At its end, you aim the car

toward Leo's dinner-place of choice,
the last rays of light
spraying our face
        in gold
        in hope
        in promise.

Moonglow

Here, in the middle
of the night,
in the middle of these streets,
moonglow glimmers,
a perfect ball of bright
filling black,
bathing streets,
illuminating the faces
of you, the people I love.

Along these concrete paths
live my father's people.
Leo searches the shadows,
looking for blanket beds
and backpack piles
and knotted forms
so he can give the hungry
our plenty, but they remain
hidden all along this way.
The Styrofoam containers
shine white in his hands.

Where are they? he says,
the night hushed around us.

And then, unexpectedly,
a hand reaches out.
Please. The word wraps us
in the worry shelling that

boy-becoming-a-man voice.
A figure, like another Leo,
steps from the dark.
Leo hands him the food,
but the boy pushes it away.
No, he says. *Her.*
And he thrusts a child
into Leo's arms. *Please.*
His eyes flash large and bright,
blazing unease
for this difficult giving.
This ain't the place for her.

The girl sleeps,
her black hair dimming
the pale blue of Leo's shirt
where her head leans
on his shoulder.
The place not for her
teems with sleeping shapes
of those too thin
and too ragged
and too rough for the
raising of a baby.

I can't, Leo says,
and he hands the girl back
to the boy. Her father?
Her brother? Another
concerned child?

Please, the boy says again,

his voice splintering now
between boy and man.
We ain't got no home.
Her daddy… Take her
before he gets back.

You step forward,
take the sleeping child
from the boy's arms.
A card flickers white
in your fingers.
Find us here, you say.

The boy shakes his head.
I can't know nothing, he says,
and then he kisses
the girl's ashen cheek
and sprints toward
the bus stop glowing red
in the starless dark.

We watch him run,
too fast to chase.
You turn to me,
your eyes stunned wide.

We can't take her, Jerry says.
She's not ours.

How do we leave her? I say,
and I take her from your arms,
feel the weight of her,

smell the dirty of her diaper,
see the beauty of this
familiar face.

The girl stirs from sleep,
violet eyes blinking at me.
She pats my face,
forehead to chin,
cheek to cheek,
and then her head falls
back to my shoulder
and her eyes flutter closed.

What do we do? Leo says.
Jerry's eyes fix on me,
and I know he has seen
and understood, too.

Take her home, I say,
and I move toward the church
where our van sits waiting
with its one empty seat
that will sit full tonight.

I turn back once to see
Leo leaving his
Styrofoam stack
for the blind girl in my arms.

Go

This way forward,
this way back up,
is not a crystal stair
but is a way crammed
with nails and sharp slivers
and timber pieces
all shredded up
and tossed before us
like a wood blanket
masking the path
we can no longer see.

Where to go from here?

There is Lily,
alerting us to a system
she spent the last
twenty-one years
of her life in,
the one with crowded orphanages
and foster home prisons
and battered children
returned to battering parents
because the blood-ties
have first claim.

There is you,
urging us to do
the honorable thing

in spite of these defects,
speaking gently
of notifying authorities
and applying for adoption
and trusting in this
structure where a toddler,
		defenseless and sightless
		and female,
does not belong.

There is Jerry,
hovering over this girl
he once pulled from that
hospital car-path
and passed back to a
heavy-handed father,
and there is a bus stop boy
with all that trust
in teenage eyes.

Where to go from here?

I watch her sleep,
morning bright
spreading through curtains
to a face still round
with baby skin.
She rests on her stomach,
head twisted to the side
and lips puckered
from the pressing.
Black hair rings

the side of her face.

You step through the doorway.
Lily stands behind you.
Her eyes find mine,
damp and soft.
She nods just barely.
Your hand warms mine,
and you squeeze
your regret.
We have to call today, you say.

I shake my head.
I can't, I say,
and those words vein through me,
throbbing their fire-rhythm.
I can't make the call.
I can't send her away.
I can't give up another.

The girl stirs.
We watch the rise
and fall of her back,
listen to the breath
holding its sleep-cadence,
and then you say,
Two days is too long.

No, I say, and my face
begins its tear burn.

Lily kneels beside me then,

slipping her arm around my waist.
We'll get her back, she says.
I know the system.

My cheeks warm with wet.
I just, I say, but I cannot finish.
You and Lily wrap arms
strong around me,
there in that bedroom
of a daughter taken from me
and another given,
the tiny girl of the
too-close kerosene jugs,
the red ball in the park,
the car-path of the hospital.

She will come back to us,
you whisper close to my ear.

How can we know
this for sure?

The girl lifts her head then,
feeling the bed with
child-tiny hands.
Mama? she says,
and it's a question gifted.
Her hands raise toward us,
and I instinctively reach
with my own and
pull her to my chest.
She pats my face

and then her smile,
with all its eight teeth,
stretches her mouth wide
and still wider.
Mama, she says, her head
dropping to my shoulder,
and that's when you
wrap your arms around
the both of us,
your eyes spilling wet
to your face and my hair.

Tell me, how do we
make that call
and send her away
and give up this girl
who already holds our hearts?

Lily slides from the doorway
and we remain in a room silent
but for our breathing,
and the boys, then,
move in and around
and into this circle of family,
the girl touching each face
and shrieking her glee
and finally breaking free
to explore her way
through this unknown house.

Where to go from here?

Giving

Giving, in the way
that we are giving,
is like a too-sharp blade
carving out good
and sealing emptiness
with a dark monstrous being.

This giving
we have known before,
with another little girl
gone too soon.

Two days become three
and then four
and then Lily urges us
to make that call,
to do it right, to hand over
and then claim back,
once time clears the way.

But this giving
is too painful and too cruel
because we have watched
the slow fade of those bruises
that purpled the plump
of her legs and we have
seen her eat soup and fruit
and those leftover beans
like she hasn't feasted

for days and we have
glimpsed her, today,
in this blue-ringed dress
with those flowers in hair
untangled and clean.

We have helped her
stumble through this house,
smiling joy at a
world so dark.
We have felt that joy
amble across the skin of us
and then grope right
down to our deeps.
We have carried her
up stairs and back
and we have set her
at the table between
Ray and Sean in a chair that
bears still the
paint-marks of Maya,
and we have laid her
in a bed unfilled
since that pool-day.

And yet, still,
you make that call,
and we follow her
through the rooms
of this house,
speaking our silent
goodbyes.

I lift her from her wobbly jaunt,
but she does not protest,
just turns her sightless
eyes toward me,
a giggle slipping from pink lips.
Her hands press my cheeks,
and I lean close with words
that used to be Maya's.
I can't promise you much.
But I can promise you
a love time will not erase.

Jerry pulls her
from my arms,
laughing at her
misses-the-mark kiss,
and then Leo takes her,
twinkling a smile
she cannot see.
You watch them
from the other side
of the room, Chris beside you
on the recliner's padded arm.

My heart thumps
its ache-rhythm
in a raw chest.
No. No. No.

I will lose another,
this one as much a gift

as the girl before her.

And then the knock
and the uniforms
and all those questions.
We tell them what we can,
mostly
          no
no we do not
know her parents,
no we do not know
the boy who gave her,
no we do not know
even her name.
Hours of questions
and answers that are
not really answers at all,
while she leans her head
on your shoulder.
Then our words: *We want her,*
and their words: *It could take
years if the court doesn't
give her back to her parents,*
and then they are gone
out the door with her
and that backpack
stuffed full of new
clothes and diapers.

This day marks
the second time
I have heard her scream

and watched her twist
in the arms that hold her.

The silence of our house
climbs around us
as we turn from the door
that divides us from her.
The flowers that, just moments
before this one,
adorned her head
stare at us from the floor,
where they fell in her
blind twisting,
the only evidence that
she has been here at all.

Lost and Found

What we have lost
lives in the room
down the hall,
where dreams were
science books heaped on shelves
and black tennis shoes
perpetually untied
and notebooks divided
by chewed pencils
left on couches
and tables and floors.

What we have lost
is in the kitchen,
where wishes were essays
penned around a
boy-scratched table
and marker masterpieces
hung from glass magnets
and that wonder wall
where her questions
waited for answer.

What we have lost
is at the pool we will
visit once more tonight,
where triumph was one toe in
and then both legs in
and then a whole body in

for those three strokes
and then ten and then
too many to count
so she'd spin around
the water like it was
all she'd ever known.

What we have lost
is out in the world, too,
where wish and wanting
are a raven-haired child
in a blue-ringed dress.

This evening is veiled,
like the eyes that watch back
from the mirror.
My gaze finds the
still-pink pucker flesh
marring my chest,
and my fingers trace
its rise and fall from collar to rib.
This
        the outer scar
mends closed,
but the inner one
is still raw
and red and leaking.

Your hand folds over mine,
resting on my wound.

You're beautiful, you say,

and I shake my head,
like I've always done
when I hear
the words I don't quite believe.

This scar won't fade, I say,
and your hand moves along
its ragged line,
lifting flesh-bumps
across my arms.

Doesn't matter, you say,
and you bend
to kiss my neck.
A camera points toward
the mirror and snaps,
the image of an image
captured in that tiny lens.
You step away from me,
raising the camera
to your eyes this time,
and you click another.

Don't, I say,
and you grin your *why*,
and in that moment,
you are the boy-man
you used to be,
back before children,
      when you spent your weekends
      snapping shoes and flower girls
      and all those college friends

vowing their adoration
while I sat in the
spectator chair alone,
sketching my *miss you.*

I thought I'd get
this old thing out, you say,
studying the buttons, fiddling.
Maybe pick up a few
photography jobs
like I used to.

You fit one arm
around my back
and straighten the other
out beside us.
The shutter closes
before I can push you away.
There aren't enough
pictures of you and me, you say,
and you show me
the frame that bears
a me staring at a you.

What we have lost
hangs there, too,
    in the lens that has stored
       the wonder of her birth
       the thrill of her first birthday
       the delight of those
         growing-up years,
   too short for the counting.

But maybe there is this, too:
What we have found
lies in that same lens
because losing
never comes without finding.

My finding is
        you and
        love and
        union stronger and wilder
                and more profound
        for the losing
borne together.

My hand slides
the camera from yours
and I kiss you on a mouth
that tastes of
                bitter-black coffee
            barely-there peppermint
        forever-always.

Begin

Dusky light fades around us.
We sit in the old
peeling-wood chairs
your dad made us,
rocking in rhythm
without really meaning to,
watching our boys
slide their skateboards
down the hill to hop the curb.
They yell and hoot and laugh,
and we pretend we do not see
the danger in this game.

Jerry sits with his girl,
her back resting against his chest,
their legs stretched straight
on one of your mother's old quilts.
I watch the two of them together,
shifting closer, his arm
wrapping around her shoulders,
her head resting
beneath his throat.

I remember that
stomach flutter
of new love,
back when
          you offered
          your hand in the dark

of a movie,
		touched my back
		on that
		rainy walk home,
	pulled up short
		so suddenly
	and dared kiss
	a girl you'd known
two days.

The wind,
like a lover's touch
to my face,
	gentle,
		soft,
			soothing,
bears on its wings
	the promise of
		fall
		restoration
		hope.
This season is our season,
one that holds within it
the offer of new life.

Here
	year after year after year
we have
begun again.

Walk with me, I say.
You follow me toward

the driveway,
past Jerry
      who's standing to join
      his brothers now
and his girl
      who smiles
      from the blanket
and up to the very
top of that hill,
where the boys collect
for another run down.

Where are you going? Chris says,
his foot staying his board.

For a walk, you say,
and Chris smiles at you,
then raises thick
eyebrows to Leo.

The moon droops
low and bright,
and before our keep-time feet
have marked the end
of the first block,
your arm wraps my back.

And my stomach flutters,
just like it did
      all those seasons ago,
      all those years ago,
      all those children ago.

Yes. I believe this is
where we begin again,
where we whisper
I-love-you words
to do-you-love-me hearts,
where we bear what may come
and rise from the fall
better and stronger
and brand new
because of it.

Different

The air hangs heavy
with morning damp,
sweet-smelling and clean
like earth just watered.
I breathe deep and long,
and then I turn toward
the woods that hide
years of our dreaming.

Lily strides beside me,
our feet keeping time
on this soft mud path
spotted with the
dried-out leaves of summer.

We walk many steps
and many minutes
and many breaths
before she speaks.

I've always loved
this place, she says.

She tells me of biking
the trails with you
in the dark of those nights
your father drank too much,
of scrambling up trees
when your mother

called you home
for too many chores,
of diving into the cool
of a swimming hole
when the heat of home-fights,
        your father arguing over
        all those acres he
        wanted to farm
        and your mother
        demanding he leave it be,
grew too warm
for the staying.

We escaped here, she says now,
her eyes on the tops
of the trees. *We used to
pretend we had different lives.*

I wonder if this is what
she pretends now
as she lowers her eyes
to the rooted path ahead,
where all those trees
reach arms toward
strong and secure.

You and I used to share
this place, too, biking the
uneven trail twists,
stealing kisses behind trees,
dipping our feet in the
cool of water.

We'd come here to
            dream.

Today you carted
your camera out the door
for a shoot, so Lily
has come instead.

We walk on, our feet
slipping through mud
and lifting over wood,
and only when we have
turned back toward the car
does Lily speak again.

I'm pregnant, she says. I stop abruptly
and then she stops, just ahead,
and turns to face me,
those clear-ocean eyes
wet with worry and agony
and unspeakable terror.
Her words a whisper:
At least for now.

I don't have any words for her,
but I open my arms
and she stumbles into them,
shaking her fear
while I shake mine,
and then we both cry for
        all those losses
        all those disappointments

and this,
          the soul-flap of hope
     that never, ever wanes.

I can't help but
love already, she says,
and I know this way of doubt
and dread and
trying-hard-not-to-hope,
this way of loving
the unknown child filling warm,
this way of hesitant
expecting and dreaming
and planning.
I have walked it, too.

Perhaps a heart in love
becomes a deep gorge,
empty to be always filled again
with the joy and trust
and possibility of this:
Perhaps this time
will be different.

Red Ball

This old park sits silent
between our home
and your father's land,
a place we'd bring the boys
when they were young,
          those years before Maya,
to fly kites and play baseball
and run trails through
the fields.

The morning stands
still and cool,
courting fall in its fingertips,
singing a sigh-song of hope
and memory and beauty.
Insects hum, birds cheer
and the sun beckons enter.

I breathe in deep
the air of remember,
and I see Sean and Ray
strapped in a stroller
and you holding a kite
and Jerry and Leo and Chris
racing behind you
for the launching
and then shouting their glee
at the take flight,
your shadows turning

brown grass gray.

Today the six of you
spread the field,
bases measured just so,
waiting for a man we met days ago
        Jim, Lily's husband,
            who took the first plane here
            when she told him the news
to hit.
Lily watches from
the sidelines.

I arrange my upright easel
and hang the canvas
from its peg
and dig in my art bag for brushes.
The eight of you make
a striking picture
against the backdrop of the sky,
and somehow I knew this
before we left this morning.

The sun hangs low
in a pink sky
when I finally step back
from the painting.

Chris stands at my elbow.
His eyes move across my canvas.
Wow, he says.

I dip the brush in some water
and wipe it with a towel.
You're up to bat now,
Jerry catching behind you
and Jim pitching.

That's incredible, Chris says.

And suddenly, I know why
I've done it.
Happy birthday, I say.

He stares at me,
brown eyes wide.
That's for me? he says.
You painted this for me?

I look at this boy
who is becoming a man
like his brothers,
who will soon join
the long line of leaving,
and those eyes,
dark and beautiful and
open wide in disbelief,
      feel the memories peel open,
      all those days wrapping
      him in a blue blanket
      in early morning dark

      carrying him down stairs
      with his head on my shoulder

so he could eat breakfast
with his going-to-school brothers

watching him master stairs
and jump off couches
and ride down hills on scooters
better and more efficiently
and faster than he should
physically have been able to

admiring his first
artistic creations
and the way he signed them
with a sideways C.

My heart twists in my chest
for the flying of these
fourteen years.

I pull him into my arms then,
my chin on his head.
I love you so much, I say,
and I kiss his brown hair.

I love you, too, he says,
and when I release him,
his eyes return
to the painting.

I wish, he says,
but he does not finish.
He doesn't have to.

I know what he wishes.
Maya loved seeing our art,
        mine and his,
no matter how good or bad.

She's there, I say,
pointing at the twinkle
of a star in my
sun-setting sky.
He grins, and then
his mouth straightens.
He points to the middle
of the picture, where Jim
is winding up a pitch.

You painted the ball red, he says,
and even though it's not a question,
I feel its wonder.

Artist's license, I say
because this secret I will keep.
I'll let it dry before I pack up.
You go finish playing.
Your team probably needs you.

And when he dashes away,
I stand back to study
this picture I've spent
all day creating.
Trapped there on a
forever baseball scene
are all the people

I love most.
You. The boys.
Jim and Lily.
Maya.

And in that red ball,
the little violet-eyed girl.

Eyes

Someone jumped
from a building
today.

Someone climbed all those
twisting rungs to the top,
sun blazing all the while
    on a face turned
        toward death
    on shoulders bent
        under *Give up*
    on legs lead-heavy
    from the moving.

Someone stood on the ledge,
raised like a caution-finger
on the lip of life,
and someone looked down
on all that grey and the
speck of his child,
and someone stepped
right into the wind.

Lily stands among the throng,
this cleanup crew of officers
and emergency responders
and child agency workers.
A two-lane street
stands between them

and the band of reporters
waiting for details.

Lily's eyes fix on a uniform face,
a man of the same team
that tried to save Maya,
and in her arms is the child
left at the building's bottom
while a father
fell from the sky.

What drives a man to fly?

Lily points toward me
and then turns with the child
whose arms wrap her neck.
She opens the back door
and slides the child in
behind me.

I need to take her in, she says.
Her voice shakes.

Okay, I say, and I open
the passenger door
and hobble toward
her driver's seat,
my after-break boot
smacking the pavement
like his skin must have done.

I shiver.

Lily meets me
at the door,
her eyes wild and streaming.
You can't drive with that boot.
Her lips curve into
a watery smile.
Sit in the back?

It's a question, a question
I could answer no,
because there is the child,
huddled in a corner,
a brown blanket pulled
all the way over her head,
covering eyes that watched
a father

      fly
      bleed
      die.

*I just don't want
her to be alone*, Lily says.

I try not to look at that
too-little lump as I
struggle into the back seat.
My breath comes hard
and fast, like my heart-pump,
and I stare ahead,
locking eyes with Lily
in the rearview mirror.

I know what she wants,
but this I cannot do.

I don't know how
to touch a child
who has seen what
this one saw.

It's not until the car
rocks into forward
and the blanket drops
from its drape
and I meet those eyes,
        the ones that will never,
        ever see anything at all,
                not even the black stain
                her father left on cement,
that I open my arms
wide.

Waiting

The mysteries of love are
       vast
       unexplainable
       surprising
like the straight stretch of grey
through flat terrain of nothing,
       on and on and forever on
until it meets a vanishing curve
that hides the sudden dropout
of land dry-brown
and gives way to
       lush green
       sloping hills
       vivid allure.

We stand at the bend
of that curve,
and we wait on next.

My love for her,
       that little violet-eyed girl,
swelled in a slow trickle,
deepening with each
chance meeting,
heaving me free from the tomb
that wreathed my sleep walk,
lining my holes with
light and breath
and new being.

As my love for her
has grown, so, too, has
      my love for you
      my love for the boys
      my love for all the people
         of my world.

This love-mystery so
      vast
      unexplainable
      surprising
breathes when you
         turn
         kiss my lips in the night-dark
         draw me soft
         into the room we claim
         and the bed we share
         and the delight we know.

It shows itself when Jerry
sings the song he wrote
      that lost-and-found one
and I can't stop the weeping
for his brilliance;

it shines when Leo
clips roses
for a dinner bouquet,
and I can't find the words
for such beauty;

it stretches when Chris
hands me the painting
he worked on all morning
                a portrait of me
and I can't speak at all
for the magnificence.

It shimmers when Sean
reads the lines Ray penned
on the way to
school this morning,
poignant words that speak of
break and empty and
filled full again.

In the days following
that building jump one,
we glean details from Lily.
The girl's mother
overdosed one night
and died in the trailer
they called home.
Her father hit the streets
but couldn't stay.
He left a note,
said he could not raise alone
a girl like her.
And then he jumped.

Her name is Ella,
but I call her Beloved
because this is who

she is to me.

She waits for claiming
inside a shelter
full of children
from backgrounds like hers.

Lily stands by the table,
stacking the official papers
in a great pile
as soon as I finish one.
*They're looking for
other relations,* she says.
*None so far.
But it could take a while.*

You squeeze my shoulder.
We'll be her temporary, you say.

I want her forever, I say.

Lily slides the thick stack
inside a folder and
opens her briefcase.
Her skin glows life,
and her belly rounds,
just barely, beneath
her flowered dress.

We just have to wait now, Lily says.

This waiting means

interviews and screenings
and extensive background
checks and a hundred
thousand other details,
just for the temporary,
and the weight of them all
rolls heavy and hard
over my neck and
shoulders and back.

What if, I say, but I cannot
finish this question
because my past
      the past of my parents
          the drugged mother
          the homeless father
stares black and harsh
and unchangeable.
Your hand closes
around mine,
warm and tender
and hopeful.

*People always want
the little ones,* Lily says.
*But she's different. Blind.
Not many volunteer to foster
children with special needs.*

Lily carries her briefcase
to the door, and I listen
to the latch-close

and the car-start
and the drive-away
before I lift my eyes to yours.
The camera hides your eyes.

This moment, you say.
This moment before we get her.

The shutter clicks,
like a starter pistol
launching us into a
waiting game.

Home

I used to believe in home
as a place, a building
        walls
        roof
        floor
a shelter where we woke
and left and then
returned and slept
    a numbered address
    on a named street.

It used to be a space
where toys and running shoes
and guitars crowded carpets
and computers covered tables
and canvases stood ready
for the painting.

It used to be a dwelling,
where we
    lived
    worked
    dreamed.

But I have learned
that home is
no place at all.

Home is you,

stirring eggs
        spooning them on plates
                serving me in bed
and home is our boys,
exploring their day-off options
        rummaging through the closet
        for that too-flat basketball
                and then rummaging
                through your tool shed
                for the buried air pump
and home is Jim and Lily,
        following us out the door
        claiming their place
        inside this crowd
                sharing our play
                and our very living and our
                deep-down-dying, too.

Home is a family,
        this circle unbroken.

Our footsteps keep time
on pavement,
eighteen feet marking
their own way forward.
The boys pull ahead,
Jerry holding the ball,
tossing it from one
to the other of his brothers.
My hobble-steps drag
you and me behind.

One of the boys says something,
and they all look back
and slow and wait.
Lily's hands rest on a belly
that curves its secret
with lines subtle still.
The skin-stretching
means nothing and yet
everything to them,
an unconfirmed promise
in light of those
ten years past.
Tragedy knows no
eighty-four-day mark or
five-month mark or
forty-week mark in their world,
like it knows no
five-year mark in ours.

Still they smile and tease
and live as if
the rest of life matters.

How does one go on living
for the waiting?

Chris walks back toward us,
a flower in hand.
For you, he says
when he reaches my side,
and I stare at this boy
who is almost a man,

at those dark eyes
so like my father's,
at that skin too smooth
for fourteen years.
I remember him at three,
when he would run those fields
        collect every flower he saw
                offer them always
                with the words,
Put them in your hair,
no matter the stem length.

And so this is what I do
because sometimes the years
and their flying
blur all that waiting,
        the waiting for do-it-yourself
        the waiting for easier times
        the waiting for freedom.

He grins as I weave the stem
behind my ear,
and then he takes my hand
and we walk on,
speaking without words.
You fall behind us,
your camera shutter clicking.

How's your leg? he asks
when we have neared
the street's end.

Almost healed, I say,
even though it beats
its pain every step
and every heart-thump.

Let me take you home, you say,
because you know
what lies between
those word-spaces.
Chris stops beside me,
his hand dropping mine.

Take her home, he says,
and then he crushes me
in a clumsy hug and lopes off
to catch his brothers.
Lily and Jim laugh up ahead,
and the boys wave.

You take my hand,
and we watch them turn
down another street.
Someone bounces the basketball,
and its smack echoes
through the canyon.

And then you lift me
in your arms and
point your feet
toward the courts
where they're headed
because you know

this truth of home, too.

Chair

The wind bursts along
the side of the house,
breathing on that chair
so it rocks,
and I could swear
I see him sitting there,
his cane propped
against his knee,
Maya's arm draping
his shoulder.

I stand in the doorway
of his house,
swept clean and
cleared out.
On the green-again lawn,
the sale sign
bends and turns,
insignificant now that
a buyer has claimed it.

I have come to say
my last goodbye.

We can't leave this chair, I say,
easing myself down into it.
I lean my head
against its smooth back
and look up at you.

You nod, your hand
sweeping the wood.
I know, you say,
and you glance toward your truck,
the truck we argued over bringing
because I prefer
the van's comfort
but you were thinking
about this chair.

And in that moment,
the overwhelm of
gratitude for you
and your always-knowing
and the sorrow for him
and Maya and all that
could have been
pulls tears down my cheeks
like a rainstorm bursting forth.
You kneel by my side,
on that cracking wood porch,
and take my hand
and pull my head
to your shoulder.

We've lost so much, I say,
words coming
between gasps.

You pull me tighter.
We've found so much, too, you say,

and the words bleed
their truth inside my deep.

I know this.

Your face is streaked
red and wet, just like mine,
by the time you draw me up
and lift that chair
and walk all those
heavy steps to the bed
of your truck.
You open the door for me,
but I stand there,
staring back at the house
that held my father
for seventeen years,
noticing the peel of the wood
Jerry and Chris helped paint
and the bushes Leo planted
while they painted
and the sticking front door Maya
could never open alone.

I breathe deep
the fresh wind
and turn away
for the last time.

Family

Who can know
the exact moment
when hope flutters in,
that unbidden thread
clinching hearts
resolute against it
for all those times before,
when it promised joy
and delivered only anguish?

Who can know
how quickly it grows
in a heart,
this light-bright that
beams through storm-black
like a pathway toward promise,
a road toward repair,
until it has already
soaked us soundly
with its flicker-glow?

Who can know
the great depths of hope,
the boundless limits of this
strong and steady feather-creature
that asks nothing of us
and yet everything of us,
that breaks free from caution
and careful and concern,

that fills, instead, with warm
and reckless and alive?

Who can know
the dark of that hope-hole
when it flies clean away?

This sharing our home
has entangled hearts
and nurtured love tender
and united our divided
into a more resilient whole.
And so we have all, unknowingly,
let hope slide its way
into our deep.

And we all feel
the ache of that cry today.

No.

You sit at the table,
reading the paper.
Jerry sits beside you,
his homework creeping
toward Leo's open notebook.
The three of you look up,
toward me, when her voice
slides beneath
the crack of the door.

No, she says again,

and the heat of hope-flight
chars my face.

Lily? I say,
my hand on the doorknob.

Oh, Erin, she says.
Please, not again.

I hear a rustle of papers,
and then you're there beside me,
prying the lock on the door,
and then I am inside, with her,
and all I can see is
the hope spilling red from a womb,
all that blood soaking
through cloth and paper and dream,
and there, in the toilet,
a too-large clump of crimson.

My heart beats cold
its *please-no* rhythm.

Not again, she says,
over and over and over.
Her eyes are wide and dry,
asking for something
I cannot give.

Who can know
how hope found
its way in again,

even after all those losses,
even in the brief of
these thirteen weeks,
even after all that trying
to block its silent slip inside?

We don't know for sure, I say,
because it's all I know to say,
and I draw her away
from all that blood,
leaving the mess in the toilet,
and you join me,
dragging her toward the car.
We ease her down
into the seat.

I'll get Jim, you say
as I close her door.

Meet us there, I say,
and you nod,
disappearing back inside.

I back out and glance once more
toward the door,
where the boys now stand,
their eyes wet and glassy,
and I see in all that brown
and the two that are violet
something I have never
seen before.

This losing
is their losing, too.

This is what it means
to be family.

I drive Lily toward help
as fast as I can,
hope still whispering weak
in this traitor heart.

Loved and Lost

The flower pots line a table,
one for every child
she's lost.

She leans on Jim,
her hand rubbing
her still-rounded belly
like a habitual reflex.
Her eyes, puffy and red
and wet even now,
move from one plant
to another, taking care
in her choosing.

I squeeze Leo's hand.
His smile is sad.

He spent all those hours
we waited at the hospital
here at home,
pouring dirt and packing plants
and trimming the dead
from the alive.
He had this surprise
waiting in the dark
when we finally
returned home.

This morning we can see

it for its true beauty.

Lily touches one plant,
a dark leafy flowering one,
and moves it to the
backyard rock-path
all these pots will line.
This one, she says,
will be Derek's.

Chris writes the name
on a smooth stone
and drops it in
the potted dirt.

Lily moves to
another flower.
Annie, she says.

And another. *Harriet.*

On and on it goes.

Eli. Sybil. Dana.
Adam. Bryan. Jill.

The pots edge our pathway
like markers on her lifeline,
and we stand before them,
marveling at their different
and their beautiful
and their fully alive

where the ones
with those names
sleep without breath.

Two pots remain on the table,
one Leo packed for Maya
and one that we don't need today,
for the baby who still grows
in Lily's warm, beside
an unexpected one who
shares the space.

So I take one and set it
beside the others.
Maya, I say.

And then I take the other,
the one I will use for the baby
the boys never knew about,
and I set it beside Maya's
where the green of their stems
wave and shift and interlock
in the wind's breath.

Pearl, I say,
and you move to my side
and take my hand because
you hear the tight of my voice,
the way it gets
just before tears,
and the tender of your touch
pulls that water forth

like a raging river
so I am choking
and sobbing
and turning into the cleft
of your shoulder.

And then Jerry
strums his guitar,
the music dancing above
and around and
deep within us,
and we stand together,
the nine of us,
in a backyard full
of the little ones
we've loved and lost,
and we watch the sun
fall below land
and the sky torch into night
and the stars glow clear
from a blue rich and dark
before we turn
back inside to celebrate
the seven of them
still here today.

Secrets

Trees hold
ancient secrets
bound tight inside
their brown arms
reaching for the blue of sky,
shivering in the wind's breath,
whispering in a
language unknown
all that they know.

I trace the rough of trunks
as I pass by,
on my way to find
you and Jerry.

I left the rest of them
in a clearing,
lounging on picnic blankets
and crunching carrots
and peeling shell
from boiled eggs.

My guitar walked off
with you and Jerry,
and so I move toward the river
you always loved for its clear water,
the same one Jerry always loved
for the first-fish-caught-and-kept
memory.

Your voices stop me
behind a tree,
just paces from the water.

*I don't want
a replacement,* Jerry says.

*No. She would never be
a replacement,* you say.

I lean my back
against the rough bark
and breathe deeply
the peace of this wood,
the bonding of the both of you,
the secrets I don't know are coming.

*Do you think we're really ready
for another?* Jerry says.

I don't know, you say.

And a blind girl, Jerry says.
*We don't even know
what to do with…* He pauses.
Blind.

Shock grips my limbs,
softening them
into burning puddles.
Panic pulls my heart,

so light and free before,
so fear-heavy now,
toward my feet,
and I follow it all the way
to the ground.
The tree holds my head
in a chilly embrace.

They are speaking of her,
the little girl we all want
and already love
and undeniably need.

Your mother wants her, you say,
but you do not say
what you want,
just let those words
hang like ropes
        chains, maybe
tightening around my throat.

Do you want her? Jerry says.
My breath snags.
I wait.

Do you? you say.
It's no answer at all.

The silence unfolds
long and weighty and bitter,
seconds trading places
with minutes while

I try to make sense of its speaking,
of your not speaking,
of Jerry's questions and doubts
and startling hesitations.

Have I steered us wrong
into this pursuit place
no one else wanted to be?
Have I moved too soon into
      mend
      repair
      move on?

Did no one else feel
the rightness of
        those violet eyes
     even though they see nothing
       that little-girl weight
     even though she is years
     younger than the one lost
       that night-giving
       and day-giving-up
     and now, today, the race
     toward forever-family?

I want Maya, Jerry says.

The wind carries those words,
so fraught with sorrow
and impossibility and longing,
straight up to the
tops of the trees

where they disappear
           into all the green fingers
and straight down
into my heart-wound,
           where they roar and thrash
           and split wide open
           what had begun
                    so slowly
to heal.

*I should have
saved her,* Jerry says.

*You did all you
could have,* you say.

It wasn't enough, Jerry says.

Yes. It was, you say.
Because you loved her.
Because you tried.

*We shouldn't have been
playing those pool games,*
Jerry says then.

They played pool games,
and I could see everyone
from that spot above water.

           I could have watched her
           skip to the bathroom

and glide back out,
        I could have seen
        the trip and the fall-in
I could have yelled
my help-cry

        but I slept instead.

And she died.

I should have stayed awake,
I whisper, and there it goes,
that secret, to join all those others
in the treetop heights.

I peer around the trunk,
tears smudging my view.
Your arms wrap him,
        our oldest son,
and both your faces
shine with sorrow
and ache and missing.

Regret can't live here, you say.
You thump his chest
with your fist,
and I feel that touch
like it was meant
for me, too.
Let it go.

Jerry reaches for my guitar then.

I wrote a song for her, he says,
his voice hoarse.
The hum of the strings
echo through the woods,
and then voice joins instrument,
        splitting and cracking
and through it all soar-singing

about a little girl who lived
in the sunshine bright
until she fell from light to dark
and closed her
violet eyes forever
        about a boy who could not save
                and a family that stood solid
                around the hole her leaving
                carved in them,
                waiting for the heal.

And long after both of you
have left this shade-place,
I sit in my hiding one,
listening to the song,
        his song,   our song,
the trees echoing it
again and again and again.

I understand their whispers now.
They say, *Healing is coming.*

Alone

I pull awake
from a sleep disturbed
by the little girl
who stands in the black
between me
and all of you.

In my dreams,
she calls to me
  pleads with those
  damaged yet beautiful eyes
   holds her hands
   straight out for the rescue,
and you and the boys
turn faces away,
and I am left there,
standing in the gap
between those
who are my family
and the one
who should be.

How do I turn away, too?

I fold back the covers,
and the cool of night
raises bumps along
the length of my
arms and legs.

You breathe deeply beside me,
and I watch your face,
young and unlined in sleep,
a half-smile shaping
your full lips.

You are near enough to touch
and yet too far away to feel.

Do you want her?
Do you not?
This is the wedge
between us tonight,
the wall raised high
between the six of you
and me
so I am
        alone
        confused
        stricken with sorrow
I can't share.

How did I miss this hesitation?
How did I read
all of you wrong?

How did I mistake your doubt
        for certainty?

How was I to know
that through it all
        the bringing her home

the giving her up
        the pursuing her again
you and the boys
held your reservations
like stones waiting
to be thrown?

Jerry's words fly
again and again,
bruising more the wounds
they marked earlier today.

And your silence
        your non-answer
do their own stoning.

I rise from the soft of our bed
and wrap my winter robe around me
and walk the dark of our house
and the dark of the sidewalk
and the dark of a street
leading nowhere.
Tonight I am a shadow
to the world that used to be
all of us together.
I drift alone
and vanish altogether
and feel the ice-cold fear
of bitter loneliness.

And yet a light,
green and blurry and unclear,

cuts the night in half,
rinsing my foot-path
in its grass-glow,
and there is Jerry, up ahead,
staring at its shine
so his face flames and sparks,
and here is me,
stepping toward him
so I glimmer with the
same bright.
He turns to me,
his eyes swollen and wet,
and he says, *She needs us,*
so I know she has
interrupted his sleep, too.

Then he takes my hand
and walks with me
back through the dark,
and I understand what I have
never understood yet before:
Alone is but an illusion,
a clever lie the mind clinches
so emotions stay veiled
and safe and unknown
behind the protection-walls
we build around ourselves.

But we never walk the dark alone
because of all we hold
folded within.

You. Jerry and his brothers.
Maya and the little girl
we will one day
call our own.

Ballots

The five of them
ring the kitchen table,
their between-gaps
equal and measured
except for the empty seat
between Sean and Ray.
We used to have
these meetings all the time,
but the effort today feels
rusty and fragmented
and uneven now,
without the one who sat
in that center chair.

I stand on the stage
of love and terror,
pacing the room
so I don't have to
watch their faces.

Their questions hang
from this ceiling
like lightless sockets
on a chandelier,
      empty
      flaking
      completing the dark
that has crept into this room
as all those secrets

crawled toward light.

Will she stay
in Maya's room?
Will she sit
in Maya's chair?
Will she take
Maya's place?

How can we move on?
How can we not?

You fold your hands
in front of you,
fingers gripping fingers.
You look from one
to the other of your sons.
I stare at the light
no one thought to
turn on an hour ago,
when we first took
our places in this debacle.

Chris presses his lips together,
then speaks in a voice
soft and raw.
She's blind, he says.
How can we—

Jerry slams his fist
on the table, his face
        smooth

            hard
            red
like that ball she chased
the first time I met her.
He doesn't seem to recall
this same question
trailing him just days ago.
She needs us, he says.

He is the only one
in this whole room
who argues my side,
this side of girl-pursuit,
and I know this by
          the shadows
          that steal your eyes
                    the straight line that pulls
                    all those mouths taut
          the rod that straightens
          their backs.

Maybe it's not
the effort of this meeting
that is rusty and fragmented
and uneven at all.
Maybe it's the seven of us,
this family that
once knew unity
and today knows
only discord.

You touch Jerry's shoulder.

Okay, you say.
Okay. We'll vote.

Jerry shakes his head
and leans back
against the rails of his chair,
arms folded across a man chest.

And they mark their ballots
in words like *not right now*
and *just not ready* and *no*
and then that one *yes,*
and I feel
        once again
the fog of bewilderment
drape my eyes
so I do not even see
all of you here at the table
but only see
        Leo
        with her in his arms
        that giving night
                Chris
                helping her downstairs
        Sean and Ray
        laughing at her face pats
the seven of us
enclosing her in our center
just before the giving up.

How could I have believed
that my fervor,

my love for that little girl,
was theirs and yours, too?

My legs move me,
lurching, out the door,
my eyes wet and blurred
and not once
looking back.

Web

The morning sun
is soft and warm,
chasing the cool
of early dawn
from the tips of my fingers.
My notebook lies
open in my lap,
but I can't find
the first word for that page
because nothing is
what it once seemed.

This love that folds
deep within my self,
is a labyrinth,
and I have walked it
afraid of the dark.

That great, intricate
web of emotion
tangles so strong
and yet so fragile,
weaving one to another
so the blind of her
became the blind of me,
and the bright breaks of sunshine
and the cloudbursts of rain
became one and the same
on this jagged path

of heal and pursue.

She needs us, I said,
        when in truth
        I needed her
        because who am I
        if not mother?

I want her, I said,
        when in truth
        I wanted a girl,
            a replacement,
        because who must I be
        without a daughter?

We'll adopt, I said,
        when in truth
        I meant that decision
        was mine.

I stare at the trees,
at the bend and turn
and redirection of those branches,
so like a life that bends
beneath its circumstances
and turns from the dark
and redirects so reluctantly
because a life must be lived
even when.

A spider silk spreads
between two branches,

connecting one to another
with those tiny lines
I didn't notice before,
without the help of sun-glare.
I squint my eyes,
studying the way it hangs,
the way it moves
in the blinking wind-gusts,
the way it whispers
that invitation, *Come,*
let us look at the world.

Steps crack behind me,
and when I turn, I see you,
staring at the web,
moving toward the bench,
dropping just beside me.
You take my hand, and we sit,
connected one to another
by the silk that is skin and bone
and fingers.

I wait for you to speak
because I know why
you have come.

Your eyes warm my face,
but I do not return your gaze.
I know what this
means to you, you say.
Silence dances on the breath
of autumn, loping around us

until you speak again.
We just need to be ready.
We just need some time.

You're right,
but I cannot say so.
The empty of that room,
        without her,
and the full of it,
        with another,
scrape the same sore in me,
but I could never tell you this
because of what it means.
But my eyes speak for me,
wetting and spilling,
and you pull me
into your arms,
your scent filling my chasm
with love and relief and calm
because we brave
this trench together
and not alone.

It's just too soon, you say.
I wanted it to be right.
You press me away from you,
your eyes holding mine.
I really did. I signed
those papers. But you heard
the boys. You know.

I look back at the web

shaking in the wind.

Yes. I do know.

We have to wait, you say.
At least for a little while.
Until we all heal.
Until we all come around.

I know this, too.

We hold our silence,
my thought-world full of boys
and a little girl lost
and another little girl
we may never see again
and we sit there
until the wind has torn
every strand of that web
away from security
so it floats on toward
a freedom unknown.

Beauty

The leaves have begun falling,
but they do not surrender gently
to the stripping of winter.
They grasp those branches
and rage against the dying
and wave the night on its way,
beckoning closer the light.

Yet they die all the same.

Where their dead fall,
they lie and wither and
crack beneath the feet of us,
      the ones who have watched
      their burning colors become
      silent brown ashes.

Where our dead fall,
we lie and wither and
crack beneath the feet of sorrow,
and our burning colors
become gray and black
and the muted white
of empty.

    Father
        mother
        brother
    daughter

how much death
can one life take?

In my fervor to move on,
to renounce the iron-hold
of anguish I have known
too intimately,
I did not realize how death
walks around us,
how the broken stalks us
like an unwanted keepsake,
how the end stands there
at the beginning, too.

The breaking widens me,
stretching my deep down
so everything feels
like another loss,
      that maddening inability
      to talk to my sons
      even though I know the rightness
      of their hesitation,
the anger like a barricade
between Jerry and his brothers,
      those papers shoved into an
      office drawer for another,
      closer-to-healed day.

And now this,
      today,
another crack in me.

It's too soon for them to leave,
but they are leaving even still,
departing for a place of their own,
moving toward a life with their family
and away from a life with us.
We need their
hope and their new,
but they need their
space and their freedom,
and so we blink and nod and hug,
and we let them go.

It's just down the road, Lily says.
She draws me out the door.
We'll walk there now,
and I raise my protest
because her belly is
large and cumbersome,
but she shakes her head
and draws me on
down the street
and then down another
and another still.

And everywhere I turn,
I see the breaks,
> in a mound of dirt
> waiting for the planting,
> in the jagged cracks
> of the sidewalk,
> in a windshield veined
> by a rock.

This is it, Lily says.
We stop beneath a
red brick house
guarded by a black iron fence,
and the broken is here, too,
      in those perfect black spikes
      and the one bent head
      in a row of hundreds.
She touches the imperfect,
one hand resting on her belly,
then pulls on the flowers binding iron.
The owner planted this
for his daughter, she says.
She died very young.
Her voice flickers, just barely.

I look at that break-gap
and the color-splash just beside it,
and I look at the grief lines on her face
and the laugh marks that ring her mouth
for the rounding of her belly,
and I look at the fire-colors of death
smoothing the way for the
new-life green on the trees
that point our way back home,
and my heart drums
with the truth.

Right here.
Right here, it says.

Broken is everywhere,
but everywhere, too,
is whole beauty.

Time

In the weeks after the vote,
I walk aimlessly around our house,
passing through every room but hers,
trying to remember what it feels like
to move forward or backward
or any direction at all.

How do we stop and stand
and still keep breathing?

Jerry sits at the table,
a school book spread open before him,
his pencil in hand.
I squeeze his shoulder in the pass-by,
but he does not lift
his black-coffee eyes
or capture my hand
like he did as a boy
or even acknowledge
I have touched him at all.

All these days
he has carried his fury
like a shield so he
huddles, alone, behind it.

This is not my Jerry,
but I don't know
where my Jerry has gone.

I turn away, into the den,
and take a book from a shelf
and drop to the couch,
where I can clearly see his face.
His eyes rake his homework.
I pretend to read.

Leo moves then,
from his chair to the
sitting-place beside me.
He doesn't speak, just sits.
I wait.

I'm sorry, he says finally,
his man-voice cracking
like the great urn
of anguish in me.
I'm sorry I needed more time.

I have no words for him,
but my arms fold
him in their circle,
and he shakes his grief
while my eyes scrape
wet flames down my cheeks.
And only when he is finished
with his pain-release
do I pull away
and look in his eyes,
more blue than violet today.

You were right, I say,
the words mine and yet
not mine at all,
spilling from a mouth
unprepared for this confession.
We all need more time.

And now there are no more secrets
nothing left to say.

Jerry slams his book shut
and stands before us in five steps.
His eyes char our faces
in their bright hardness.
She doesn't have time, he says,
and then he pitches
out the front door.

And Leo and I
watch the door
for a good long while,
but it remains
      closed
      sealed
      locked to this life
of winds and tides.

Wings

Before our lips
knew little else
but somber sounds,
before the melancholy
numbed our throats
and our limbs and our souls,
before this woe leeched
our hearts of pleasure,

                there existed a place.

You have driven us
to this stretch of land
we know only in memories
because the years,
       the way they grew our boys,
separated us from its play
long before Maya learned
to walk and run and swing.

I heard the way
your voice thickened
around your words, *Get in,*
and I saw the way
your hands shook
as you pointed the car
toward the surprise only you knew,
but I never would have guessed
your mind had wandered here.

You order us out of the car,
your words climbing
free behind us.
Maybe we'll remember.

We step on a ground
dim with shade
and stare at those black tires
hanging from limbs still
thick with life even
in the midst of death.
The wind whispers
through the leaves,
like an invitation.
Tell me your sorrows, it says,
but where do we even begin?

You stand before all of us
     fling your arms wide
        say, *What can we remember?*

Leo is the first to speak.
Peace, he says. You nod.

Hope, Chris says.

Life, Jerry says. *How to live.*
His eyes rake the ground.
My eyes search his face,
but it remains closed to me still.

Joy, Sean says.

I miss joy, Ray says,
clutching the arm of his twin
until they both move,
their steps even and quick,
toward one of the swings.

Your eyes lock with mine.
Trust, you say, your voice faltering.
And then it is my turn
to speak of what has been lost
and what must be found again.

Who am I? I say, though I
never meant it as a question.

You come to me then,
binding me in arms warm and strong,
and the memories flash
across the black of my mind-screen,
        the day you first sang
        that parting-song and I cried
        over its truth
                the day you crouched
                by my bedside in the night-dark
                so you could make sure
                my fever had cooled
        the day you offered a ring
        and your name and forever.

I have always,

always loved you.
Maybe I have never
told you this.

When you have held long enough,
you move toward Chris and Leo,
who claim a second swing,
and I am left with only Jerry,
standing alone in a patch of dirt.
He stares at his brothers,
his eyes tracing their
circle-flight through air.
I move to his side
and take his hand in mine,
the sounds of your
laughter and theirs
shifting within like a
long-forgotten melody.

We stand there
a good long while,
watching the swings
sway and pitch and loop,
watching his brothers
push and ride and shout,
watching you breathe deep
their warm delight,

and then Jerry says,
*I just don't know
how to let her go.*

I stare at the leaves
above my head,
waving from their
great heights, and I feel
their gentle flutter in my deep,
in the place where the grief of her
meets the joy of them,
and I squeeze his hand tighter.
Together, I say.
We learn together.

We sink to sit on grass,
and I tell him, then, of
  a grandfather who
  lived a storied past
    a grandmother he never met
  an uncle, long dead and gone.
I tell him of
  a sister he never knew
    another who used to fall asleep
    on his shoulder every time
    he asked to hold her
  who said his name first
  of all the brothers
who loved the songs
he sang most of all.

He listens and he weeps,
his tears dropping to earth
like pearl beads falling
from a costly string.
And when he has finished,

the wind dries the wet
with fingers deft and chill and hopeful,
carrying on its breath
an enchantment that lifts him
from his ground-seat
and launches him toward
the closest tire swing,
still vacant because
you have all been
waiting for him.

He wraps his legs around rope
at the same time you wrap
father-arms around his chest,
and then you push him away,
high toward those limbs shaking
now in the laughter of his flight,
and his brothers join the joy-noise,
the ones on the ground
racing between the ones in flight
so by the end of it we're all
weeping and laughing
        like ones who once had wings,
              like ones who will find them again.

Numbers

There is one place
I did not dare go.

In all those days
after her dying,
I walked the floor
of the library
strung with butterflies
and swathed my melancholy
in a silent breath
that shook them ever so gently,
ever so surely.
I retraced our walks,
counting steps to the
stop sign and back again,
smashing ear against the
tree trunk for a nature listen,
collecting trash-treasure
like she always did.
I stared at the blue of the pool
and watched children
splashing and playing,
and I gripped those
pointed iron rails,
so cold and unaffected,
to steady my shaking
because I could not see
the clear of water
without seeing, too,

the black hair cloud
that wrote death
across that cement bottom.

I tracked all those places
where she walked and
played and lived,
but I did not come here.

I park in the lot
and slip through the doors
and wander down the hall
of this learning place
        because I must
        because she still lives here
     because her living
     is like a concrete block
     bound to my heart
     by knotted string
dragging behind me
bleeding me of my heal-victory.

Every step toward the door
that swallowed her
every Monday and
Wednesday morning
is like another tether falling.

And then a wall
colored by numbers
stops me short.

One
the number that speaks of
        only daughter
        missing,
        gone forever and ever and ever.

        Two
the number that chases
        our walks there and back
        our steps left and right
        our conversations whispered
        between mother and daughter.

        Three
the number of all those
crayon-scribbled doors
marking the rooms
of our house.

        Four
the number that says
she knew
        how to put on her shoes
        how to ride a bike
        how to swim.

        Five
the number of her years
        the number of too young
the number of too soon gone.

        Six

the number of once upon a time
        when all my children lived.

        Seven
the number that tells us
how long we waited for her
and who we are now
        without her.

        Eight
the number that remembers
who we used to be
        before the losing.

        Nine
the number she chose
as her can't-wait-until-I'm.

        Ten,
the number that wears
the whole truth of it
        how one becomes zero
        and something becomes nothing
        and daughter becomes dead.

I stand there with bowed head,
my eyes counting and recounting
the numbers that are her numbers,
and I weep
        as if the tragedy
        has only just begun,
as if the clouds of calamity

have only just spit their malice,
        as if the heart-bleed
        has only just gushed its grief.

I press the jagged scar
atop my heart
as if the pressing will stop
the beating pain there.

And then I sit,
the gulf growing wider in me,
until a hand
        warm
        soft
        hospitable
pulls me to my feet.
A face,
                one I know,
swims nearby, and then
arms enfold me
in fleshy softness.

She draws me into a small room,
where child art papers the walls,
and she talks about
a brilliant little girl
who died too young
and a mother's heart
that heals around the hurt
but never quite forgets,
and it's not until she's finished
that I understand she is not speaking

of Maya and me.

'Where beats the human heart
she felt cruel pain,' she says.
You know Keats, I'm sure.
She shifts in her chair,
her eyes holding mine.
That's what mother sorrow is.

I cannot speak or move,
but she rises from her sitting-place
and turns to a shelf.
I kept some things, she says.
I thought you might
like to have them.

I nod and take the box,
my limbs cold and stiff.
She walks me to the doors
and holds one open.
When I move silently past, she speaks again.
The missing lasts forever,
but hope always wins, she says.

Her words trail me to the car,
where I bend and twist
for the agony of that name
     written in capital letters still
and a Mother's Day card
she never had the chance to give
     a picture of me linked to her
     and that red wagon beside us

and a thought balloon above us
        declaring forever-love
and that poem about you
        a daddy who liked to dance
        and prance and wear nice pants.

I slide those riches
back in their treasury
and fumble my way home
to you and the boys
and what we must
do from here.

Shadow

Her shadow walked into our home
and sat in all the rooms
and bent our shoulders to breaking,
and we have carried it too long.

So we are giving it back.

We gather in the room
where she slept for
five short years.
Her window opens
to a troubled sky,
gray like our hearts.

We do not know
where to begin,
but somehow we do.
Jerry moves to the bed,
stripping the covers
that I did not wash
in the days or weeks
or months after her dying
because I needed the scent of her
        that sweet lavender
a living child trapped
in cotton fibers.

I turn away, and behind me
Leo stuffs all those animals

she called friends
into a white trash bag.
Their eyes stare at me through plastic,
speaking a terror that feels
too much like my own.

Chris stands at the stone wall,
tracing the lines of his mural.
His cheeks shine wet.

Sean has pulled all the boxes
brimming full of her art
and writing and all those
random pieces she couldn't
bear to throw away,
from beneath her bed.
They are treasures now
because it's all we have left of her.
Ray kneels beside him.

You stand at the closet,
and from your hand
hangs one of the sandals
    once bright red but now muted
    like the world without her
she wore until the soles
turned paper-thin.
Your eyes speak what
none of us can say.
How do we do this?

How do we say goodbye?

I move to your side,
but you do not shift
or blink or speak.
You just stare at that shoe,
where the impression of
        her feet
              her toes
                    the heel she touched first
                    to the ground
still remains.
I gently peel your fingers from it
and bend to place it in the box
where her things will go.
When I rise, the room swims
for this lost piece of her.

You look at the clothes again
        long line of shirts
        and dresses and pants
        and the unworn ones
        stuffed in the back
        because she wanted to save them
        for this year's family photo,
              only death
        claimed her
first.

I begin to take them all down
        one by one
hangers and all,
stuffing them into the box

that will carry her shadow
from our home.
I try not to see them
for what they are,

but there is the shirt she wore
to her last birthday party
     and there is the jacket she wore
     last Christmas
          and there is the dress she wore
          to her last dance with you.

You take the dress from me,
pressing it against your face,
and you crumple to the ground
bending beneath the remembering.
It was just days after wearing this
that she floated at the bottom of a pool.
Your sobbing draws us to your side,
my arms spanning the broad of you,
your sons filling the holes.

When your breath evens,
we help you to your feet.
Sorry, you say, the first words
any of us have spoken
in this room today,
and we all shake our heads
because sorry does not belong
in this black of death,
     where papers and dresses
     and sandals worn every day

for months on end
tell of the beloved one
we have lost.

You join me in work again,
and we lift and stack methodically,
side by side, the silence
encasing us in its sadness.

After we have finished,
        when we have pulled
        all those clothes from the closet
        and out of drawers
    when we have stacked
    her treasure boxes
    on the uppermost shelves
    for safekeeping
we turn to the window
that is weeping like us,
and we stand there statue-like,
locking our fingers
around the hands of one another
because we must do this
heart-aching giving,
        this difficult work of letting go,
    this final farewell
together.

Goodbye, sister, they say,
their voices shifting
around the barb of it.

Goodbye, daughter, we say,
and our voices crack thick and deep,
right down to the hollow in us,
and we watch the rain
mark the window
like it marks our cheeks.

You and Jerry lift the box
heaping with her belongings
      the one that holds
      our goodbye-words
      and the shadow of her
      between all its sorrow-folds
and you heave it down the stairs
and pack it in the back of our van,
and when the rest of us
follow you out and slide into seats,
we see that the sun
has broken through the gray,
laying bare a sky
blue with invitation.
Come, let us finish
this work, it says.
So we drive toward
the place of rest.

Dawn

We have walked the path
of this resting place
only once since her
burying day.

The sun has dried
rain's water-beads
by the time we brave it again.
Musty earth-odor
wafts around us,
turning our minds
to the day black soil
sprayed the top of her casket
and slipped down the
still-glossy sides.
I closed my eyes against the
forever-covering that day,
but I could still hear
the drop of those grain-pieces
that would seal her
in the dark womb of earth.

We stop before her stone,
unbearably white in the glare
of the sun's last light.
The tulips Leo planted
that other day bend and
wilt before her grave,
like sorrow shoots.

Leo stoops to pull
the weeds choking
her favorite flowers,
then turns the dirt
just beside them,
carving the hole
where he'll put
the rose bush he
carried here today.

I brought some roses, he says,
as if she can hear him.
He plants the bush deep,
all of us watching,
and then packs the soil in place
and sits back on his heels.

Jerry kneels beside his brother,
an arm resting on Leo's shoulder.
I watch the brothers
bow their heads,
and I swallow the
thickness in my throat.
Your arm circles my waist.

Chris and Sean and Ray
flank the two oldest then,
and they all five kneel there together,
        these brothers who have
        lost their only sister.
Their breaths rise and fall

                rise and fall
and their shoulders
shake the truth of their pain,
telling of the ache not-yet-healed
and the loss not-yet-forgotten.

Will we ever heal?
Will we ever forget?

Only breeze-whispers
break the hush all around.

When enough time has passed,
you and I join them,
kneeling before her death-stone,
where damp dirt wets our knees
and drooping tulips
lend color to grey
and red roses loose their petals
to dance on wind-breath.

The trees sigh.
Sleep, my love,
my daughter, they say.

The sky in front of us explodes,
firelight burning blue
with gold and crimson,
charming night-veil
toward the sky-top.
The sun flees black
while we watch,

but its memory blazes on
in my heart, and it's only then
that I see it with fresh eyes,
with a wiser heart.

Night is nearly finished,
and dawn will come again.

The first star
gleams soft.

Whole

Today I close my studio door
and open the four windows
so the cold snakes into warm
and I paint.

Color floods white
in stroke after stroke,
parting and then joining,
tinting a canvas complete.

Time writes it impassively,
all those emotions claiming colors,
and I am but a
silent observer.

My hands finally still,
no work left to be done,
and I step back. The sun beams
through the window,
hours gone in a few minutes.

I feel you before I see you,
eyes burning my back. I turn.
You stand in the doorway,
a piece of paper in hand.
Your eyes move to my painting.

Wow, you say.
You did that today?

I face the easel again,
a smile scorching my deep.

Might this be a masterpiece,
all hope and emotion and
redemption in color?

The silence softens around us,
and then you step into the room.
You press the paper into my hand.
I missed our anniversary, you say.
So I wanted to give you this.

You shut the door
behind you.

Shadows creep into the room,
day almost done.
I spread the paper in my lap,
your handwriting scrawled
small and precise on a
front and a back.
The words begin clear,
then blur as I read on.

She rises from the past,
that woman I used to be,
shaped by the words
you have given me.
Shadow woman
      this me today

moves silently to meet
her.

And when the shadow has waved
goodbye to the whole left standing,
I turn back to my canvas,
to paint the words you've written,
the ones that remind me who I am.

I paint them
across my masterpiece
until that color palette
shines empty.

Twilight

Behind the gates of our home
we sit, winter's twilight
still and hushed around us.

The twins stand,
because they have to,
because we're all singing,
and they look like
tiny power lines
against a flaming sky,
bound one to another
by all those mysterious
cords of brotherhood.

For a moment, the sun
forgets to run toward rest,
and all I see before me
are those too-tiny babies
with lines from their noses
and feet and chests
and a clear-sided sleeping-box
and a heart monitor
flashing those numbers,
1
      4
         3.

I love you,
    that's what it said,

right there on a
scientific screen.

Because I had never
left a hospital
without a baby,
and that day I did.

It was the darkest day
I had ever known then,
but life had much darker
ones planned.

And yet, here we are,
celebrating them today,
in fold-up chairs
circled around a fire
in our backyard.

We have lived our twilight,
and we have lived our midnight,
and we carry on,
toward the dawn.

Those clouds. Sean points.
The head of a dinosaur.

It was a game they
played with Maya.
We all have our turn
in what light remains,
staring at the clouds

and speaking our sightings
and glancing toward the
garden-corner, where her plants
have given up green
for the cold.

I shift my chair closer to the fire,
cold stiffening my fingers.
You move yours closer to me,
your arms finding my shoulders,
rubbing them warm.

The sky sings
its goodnight lullaby,
a pink and orange
and shimmering blue song,
but we do not rise
when the sun dips
and black swallows
its sky-blaze. Sean and Ray
have asked for a campout
to mark their twelfth year.

And after we cook
dinner over flames
and slice cake to eat
and roast all those
marshmallows to flatten
between chocolate,
we climb into our tents,
under layers of blankets
        the boys in one

        you and me in another
and we sleep by the
light of the moon.

The black sky
        all its glittering stars
might have told us
what came next,
but it remained
as silent as the
winter wind.

Rise

When I wake,
it is still dark.

The wind does not
rest this morning
like it did last night.
Our tent shivers,
but you do not stir.

I hear it again,
what pulled me
from sleep. A name.
My name.

The backyard is
dim and shadowed,
but a light spills
from the back door.
Lily stands in the doorway,
her belly larger for the
glow behind her.

I move quickly.

Something has happened, she says
when I'm close enough to hear
the hush of her voice.
I would have come last night, but…

She glances toward the backyard,
then turns to sit in a chair.
I sit across from her.

Her eyes hold no worry,
only uncertainty.

*It's about the little
blind girl,* she says. *Ella.*

I grab her wrist.

She's okay, Lily says,
and then she pauses,
her eyes searching mine
as if they hide answers
to questions she has
not asked.

We found more family,
she says then.
We found the father's sister.

The words twist tight
around my heart
because even though
we decided to wait,
even though we knew
something like this could happen,
I thought she was ours.

So that's it? I say.

Ella's father had a sister, Lily says,
as if she hasn't heard me.
She leans close.
You, Erin.

The heat of her words floods me,
        spinning the room
                suspending the minutes
        blacking my vision
                until all I see is that tiny body
        lying in a closet
dead.

No, I say. *He died.*
He was a baby. I saw him,
dead on the floor.

She does not know what I saw
beside the room
where my mother slept,
one pocked arm
flung over her eyes.
Blue lips. White skin.
Still breath.

I left home after
police cars swarmed the house,
after all those child experts
questioned me,
after they carried his
little blanketed body out the door.

I left because I knew
where they would put me
and what it would do to me
and what better I could
do for myself.

My brother
        alive
left to my mother and…
        what?
How could I have known?

Lily shakes her head. *Your brother
had a daughter.*

She tells me about this
brother I never knew,
how he
        cared for my mother
        in her old age
                saw his daughter's mother
                die of an overdose
        left that suicide note
        saying he could not deal
        with all that death
and so chose to join
the ones he loved.

What if I had known him?
Would that have saved him?

Why didn't I know? I say,

and it is something
neither of us can answer.

My eyes blur.
We sit in a long silence,
until morning's first light
burns gray-blue.

She'll be yours, Lily says.
Whenever you're ready.

I nod, and she rises to go.
When the front door closes behind her,
I move to the porch
and sink into a chair
backed against the railing
you built years ago.

Just beside me is a plant
        brown and withered
reaching one still-green
finger toward me.
Something survives
this winter of death.
I touch those leaves
and feel their hope
stir my deep.

I sit and listen
for the first birdsong
and wait for you
and the boys to rise

with the sun.

Cracks

I know the beginnings
and the ends of things,
    the birthing of babies,
    the dying of one.

I am beginning to know
life after the end.

We lived once upon a time
like a habit, and then it ended.
We stretched and cracked
and yet we did not
come apart.

And now we stand, once more,
at the bottom of a rising climb
because all we know
to do with blind
is love.

Today we will
step upward together.

Jerry peers out the window,
afternoon glow reaching
across the front lawn.
Of all of them,
he cried most that
morning you all woke

and I spoke.

It all happened so fast,
the story telling and
the six of you agreeing on now
and then the knowing
we would get her
before the year's end.

Lights glitter from the tree.
Christmas has come and gone,
but we left it there,
pushed up against a window
overlooking our backyard
because this day is our Christmas,
a day when a little girl
becomes ours.

A girl who lost her family,
and we who lost our girl.

A flower like she wore
her leaving-day sits on my knee,
ready to find its place
in her black curls.

You sit beside me on the couch,
your eyes gripping the floor.
I look at you,
and then they grip mine.

How will I love

another daughter? they say,
and I cannot answer
this for you.

Time becomes audible
in these moments
before her arriving,
        in Leo's foot tapping
        in the breathing of
                Chris beside me
        in Jerry's finger
                against the window.

And then it stops completely,
like a breath held before the fall,
when Jerry says, *They're here.*

You rise from the couch,
pulling me with you,
and it's all like a misty dream.
My heart flutters
                then slams
then flutters again.

Jerry opens the door,
and there she is,
the little girl we have
awaited these silent hours.
She is smiling, dimples
clefting her cheeks.

No one can even speak.

And then it's you
      lurching forward,
      brushing the shoulders
         of your sons with a
         courage-hand
you she hears first.
Welcome home, Ella, you say,
and she reaches
for your voice.

The cracks give way inside,
and I weep for the beauty
of all that has come before
and all that stretches ahead.

Hope

At long last,
our twilight has
recovered the
blush of dawn.

Winter passed,
carrying spring in a
torrent of rain, and today,
this day that marks
Jerry's graduation day,
the world beams green
and blazing bright
because of those waters.

We gave up much,
and yet we need
nothing more.

Ella fit our family
like she had
always belonged,
like we walked
incomplete without her,
like the hole carved by death
waited for another life.

If Maya had lived,
would this rhythm
have beat the same?

Would there have been Ella?

I cannot answer this for certain.

But Ella is here today,
perched on your knee,
four of her brothers beside us,
completing Jerry's cheering crowd.
The last one stands on stage,
summoned to speak.

He faces
a crowd of thousands,
but he looks only at our row
        at brothers and sister
        and aunt and uncle
        and mom and dad.
The whole room
waits to breathe,
one collective breath
holding for Jerry.

He clears his throat,
hands clenched to both
sides of the podium.
My hands bend into fists
because he is my son
and this is agony.
You peel my hand loose
and wrap our fingers
together.

And then he begins,
in a voice strong and
sure and confident.

He speaks of her,
        of a black death and how
        he tried his best to save,
                how the hole of death
changed the whole of his life.

He speaks of a beloved sister,
        of cuddle-hugs and love-drawings
        and an empty seat in the car
        and at the table and in his heart.
He speaks of
                sorrow
                regret
                anger
at life after the end.
He speaks of himself,
like a churned-up river,
        turned aside by the
        rocky life-shores,
                pressed into a trench
                he would never have
                chosen willingly,
erupting into the stillness
of a pool where light
burst through dark.

He knows the way
the darkness holds the light

of a resurrected marriage
    a restored life
        another little girl
        with violet eyes.

He speaks of what
he should not yet know
in all his years.

By the time he is finished,
there is not a dry eye
in the room.

But every heart here
wings on hope.

After

We come here almost as if
it were our home.

Many times in the last year,
we have walked this same way,
but today freedom lifts its head
and takes notice.

Songbirds lilt and twitter
in the evening warmth,
lining the path with music.
Summer's breath
puffs through trees
so their leaves whisper
and clap and keep time
with birdsong.

We stand, eight strong,
just before the white stone
marking Maya's earth.
Jim and Lily wait in the distance,
each holding a promise-child.
The sight of them,
those babies peering
from parent-arms,
pulls a smile from my heart.
I turn back to the rock
where our own promise-child rests.

Ella's head drops to my shoulder.
She points ahead of us.
Sister? she says.

Is it the feel of this walk
she recognizes, or is it the
feel of us?

Leo pats her back,
then steps forward
to snap a bud from the rose
bush he planted here.
He cuts the few thorns
and then tucks it
behind Ella's ear.
She touches the bloom
and smiles.

The sun beams
on all our faces,
and its warmth
spreads down deep.

She lives still,
in the bedroom that has
become her sister's,
in the chair kept empty
in a kitchen corner,
in the doorbell chime
you fixed.

She lives still in all of us,

in the love that binds us
surer and tighter
and stronger than ever before.

The rains have come and gone,
and now summer grins its light,
drying all those sorrow-waters
so we can finally see
above their surface again,
        so we can plod our
        slippery way forward,
                so we can step onto new
                and different and
                startling shores.

We can feel it in our hearts,
freedom's invitation.
Come. Move on. Live again.

And so we do.

I look at you,
                at the gray that has
                spread through black,
        at the eyes still shadowed,
at the wrinkles cut by suffering,
                lines that will never leave,
and I can see how our faces
fell apart in the middle of it all,
        but you are still mine
        and I am still yours,
and this is still

                    forever.

I take your hand.

They are so tall
Almost men.
        Jerry
will be the first to leave us.
A bitter ache knots in my chest.

It's not just the forever-leavings
that feel hard. But they are
the only leavings
that can teach us
how to stand.

Leo brushes my hand,
his eyes silent questions.
I nod. He moves
toward his brothers,
and they all open their hands,
where red petals have waited
for the letting go.
They dance on the wind
like the ashes of my father.

And when we have watched
the last of them flutter away,
we turn back, together,
toward Jim and Lily
and those babies shining hope.

In hindsight we can see it
more clearly,
how after every sorrow,
joy came back again.

Hush

The months move on
      one after another
and before we know it,
another year is ending,
and we haven't seen Jerry
in two months.

One day, a week before
we mark the day she came to us,
I am walking out the door
for a mid-morning run,
and Jerry stands on the doorstep.

He is much taller than me now,
and stronger, more a man
than when he left,
but I fall into his arms anyway,
my head resting against his chest.
His heart thumps a steady beat
into my ear, and my eyes blur.

I'm so glad you're home, I say,
and he tightens his hold.
We walk through
the door together.

Jerry! his brothers shout,
but it's Ella who reaches him first.
She loved him most, of all of us.

He crushes her in big-brother arms,
and she pats his face,
her eyes shining violet.
He grins and kisses her cheek.

You wrap him in arms
as thick as his.

His brothers hug him, too,
all of them, and then we
sit in our living room,
talking for hours of
all he's missed
and all we've missed.

Leo tells him of the tree out back,
the tree he saved from dying,
and Chris shows him
the stacks of paintings he's done.
Jerry picks the one
with a yellow-white moon
glowing on black water
to take back with him,
        a Christmas present, he says.

Ray and Sean ask for stories
of his new college life,
and Jerry tells them,
        one about a roommate
        who lost his father
        and how they walked through
        the grief of it together

one about a class he enjoyed
more than any other
one about a special
girl he's met.

His voice changes
when he speaks of her,
and you wink at me.
My heart clenches around
another bittersweet arrow
aimed just right.

The conversation winds down,
and I leave all of you sitting there
so I can trace the route
I've run for almost a year now.

I barely notice my legs burning
as I climb uphill, so lost am I
in thinking of this year we've had
and the one before it
all the hell and the heaven
all the dark and the light.
So much pain
and yet
so much bliss.

Can we recognize heaven
without hell
light without dark
bliss without pain?

If
        from that old life
I could step outside myself
and see my today-life
I would know surely that only
in the sorrow-prison coming
would the dry and arid
turn soft and alive,
        would we finally
        begin to discover
                what it means to live free.

Hell dragged us
all the way to the bottom,
and love lit the way
back up.

I breathe and pound my way
to the floor of the hill,
and there you wait,
the car pulled to the
side of the road.
Two drinks sit on its top.
I stop, my breath
coming in gasps.

Drink? you say,
and you hold it toward me.

I nod. It's hot chocolate
with peppermint,
too sweet and warm

to drink right now,
but I sip it anyway.
We stand in silence
until you set your cup down again.
I wanted to show you something, you say,
pulling your guitar from the back seat
and slinging it over your shoulder.

I haven't heard you play
in too many years,
and already I feel
the emotion choking
my throat.

You sing me a familiar song
I've never heard before,
  about a girl who walks blind
  until she learns to see
  with her heart
    about a girl lost and found
about a girl who always
belonged but never
really believed it
    until love led her home.

At first, I think it's a song for Ella,
but the music widens around me,
sinking into my invisible holes,
and then I know.

It's about me.

The strings shake still,
their hum quiet now.
You stand staring at the sky,
and then you push
your guitar to your back
and pull me to your chest.

Beautiful, I say,
and I am not just speaking
of the song.

Your arms fold me
in love and warmth and life.
My eyes wet your jacket,
and you bend to kiss
my forehead.

We heal in the hush,
and it is
      final and
         complete and
miraculous.

The End

In the end,
you were the only one
who truly found freedom
from the burden of days.

We would have
twenty-three more
good years with you
before your mind
would wander away,
before you would not
be able to say,
with any certainty,
who Jerry or Leo or Maya was,
before you would sleep
with childlike soundness
in our still-shared bed
while I would write our story
by candlelight.

I would write because
in those to-be days,
you would forget
all that time bent
and unbent in us,
all the space between
now and the would-be.

In the future,

we would begin every morning
at our used-to-be-full table,
where I would sit
holding your hand
and you would sit
listening to the best
parts of our lives,
because I could never
read you the hard ones.

We would ease our days
through six journals,
and when we finished,
we would do it again,
and I would begin
all those readings
with Dear Phil,
because that's what you
have always and ever
been to me.

Tonight, the evening stands still,
except for a little girl
twirling the dance floor,
clutching a daddy's hand.
She misses all those steps,
but she beams all the same
because your arms
hold steady and strong.

You lift her in the air,
this beloved daughter

blind to the world's color,
and I see joy beaming
in her violet eyes.

Under our gaze
this journey unraveled,
a road long and solemn
and agonizing, and yet
we did not yield, and somewhere
along the way it turned
unexpectedly beautiful.

Hope walked before us
toward a brand new day,
and we followed
without looking back.

In all my searching,
I have found no words
to express the loveliness
of loving well.

I only know this:
Love always stands
at the end of everything.

THE END

About the Author

Rachel is the author of the poetry books, *this is how you know*, *Life: a definition of terms*, *The Book of Uncommon Hours*, *Textbook of an Ordinary Life*, *this is how you live*, *Sincerely Yours*, *Textbook of a Parenthetical Life*, *Textbook of an Extraordinary Life*, and *this is how you fly*; the middle grade books, *The Colors of the Rain*, *The Woods*, and *The First Magnificent Summer*; and multiple essay collections as well as books for children under a pen name. She has been writing poetry since the time she could hold a pencil and form what passed for letters on the page. Her first introduction to poetry was the brilliance of Shel Silverstein, whom she still reads today.

Her poems for children and adults can be read in literary magazines and online publications around the world.

Rachel lives with her husband and six sons in San Antonio, Texas. She daily reads poetry (as well as many, many books) to her children, because poetry, she says, contains the essence of life, and reading, she says, is the gateway to a future of promise.

In the End is her first adult verse novel.

Author's Note

My dear reader,

This book began many, many years ago, when I partnered up with my good friend and photographer, Helen Montoya Henrichs, for a yearlong project to rekindle the passion we felt for our art. Helen and I met at the *San Antonio Express-News*, when I was a young reporter and she was a young, extremely talented photographer. Over the years, we had both shifted into jobs that didn't use our skills and talents quite as much as we would have liked, so one day I asked her if she wanted to collaborate on a project together. She would provide the photos, I'd provide the words.

For the entire year of 2012, Helen sent me two photographs every week. I used them to write my poems that would connect into a story. Then I shared them with readers on my blog.

I don't know how many followed along with that story way back then, but I do know the consistent practice of writing two chapters of a story every week launched me back into my writing career and showed me it was possible to create in the tiny little spaces of life, with tiny children often stealing my time and attention.

During that year of writing *In the End* (the original title was *Violet Shadows*, but the more seasoned writer I am today recognizes that title as a bit, well, melodramatic) I had newborn twins, and three other children four years old and younger. None of them were in school or daycare. Five children dominating my time. This project became a me-project. A lifeline of hope. A remembering of who I was. You will see threads of that in the story, particularly in the poems, "Shadow Woman" and "Whole."

Between 2012 and 2014, I tried to get this book published. But it was rejected countless times, because it was an adult novel written in verse. "Adults don't want to read a book in poetry," one agent told me. Another said editors would laugh their asses off if she pitched an adult novel that was less than 80,000 words (*In the End* is a little more than 40,000 words). So I put the book away. For years!

A couple of years ago I pulled it back out, decided I would share it with the world—my own way. I polished, cut a few things, but basically left the story as it originally appeared. And while I may have, today, done things differently than I did all those years ago—twelve years; that's how long it's been since I wrote this book—I've chosen to honor this story as past me recorded it. Because it's a great story. And past me was exploring big ideas like love and forgiveness and loss and hope, and those things are just as relevant and important today as they were then.

I know what it's like to lose a daughter—not in the same way Erin knows it in the story. But I understand the depth of that grief. The way it cracks you to pieces. How you're not sure you'll make it. And I know that if we just look hard enough, we'll see the light slanting through the cracks. Life goes on, and we go on with it, one day at a time.

Dark never lasts forever. Hope lights the way out.

Keep holding tight to hope.

Acknowledgments

This project began as a collaboration between me and my photographer friend, who faithfully sent me two superb photos every week for a whole year. So I must first and foremost thank Helen Montoya Henrichs—not only did your photographs do wonders for my creativity, but they were beautiful works of art I still have on my computer hard drive. Is it weird that I sometimes take them out and imagine these characters in the landscapes, smelling flowers, running trails, observing buildings? Probably.

Ben, you have always been an encouraging partner in every part of life, but for this particular project, I remember your frequent, "I'll put them to bed myself. You go write." This story would not have amounted to much without you. (Do you remember how exhausting it was to daily care for a four-year-old, a two-year-old, a one-year-old, and newborn twins? I want to take a nap just thinking about it! But also—where did those years go?)

Jadon, Asa, Hosea, Zadok, Boaz, and Asher—where would I be without you, without your love, without the laughter you carve out of every space in the world? This story certainly could not have been written by me without your presence showing me the heights of love that could amount to deep dark depths if I had to lose any one of you. I love you so very, very much, even if our house does now smell like a boys' locker room where certain people forgot their deodorant. You are my sunshine.

Sam—when I'm at my depths, you always have a kind word and encouraging truth to pull me back out. Thank you for your gratitudes and for being you. For cheering me on and reminding me of hope. Sisters don't always share blood.

Alana—it's friends like you who keep me standing strong during the storms in life. Thank you for believing in me and reminding me it's not selfish to do what you know you were made to do.

My blog readers, way back when—thank you for following along and loving this story as much as I did.

And you, dear reader—thank you for sticking around for the credits and reading my story. I hope you found yourself somewhere in these pages and that you remember you deserve every good thing, especially a love that lights the dark.

Enjoy more titles
from Rachel Toalson

racheltoalson.com

www.ingramcontent.com/pod-product-compliance
Lightning Source LLC
Chambersburg PA
CBHW061542190726
48289CB00004B/1137